The *sake* hit Abigail all at once. The street was awhirl with colors: blue robes, green *sake* bottles, bronze beer cans, yellow banners, red flags, rainbow-colored fans. London was in front of her, down the road, carrying a gold shrine. The muscles in his back flexed with his movements. She allowed her eyes to drop to his hips.

She felt drunk already.

And tomorrow was work.

And there were no promises about what her future would hold.

But tonight? Tonight she'd be with him.

NIHON NIGHTS

TRISHA HADDAD
and
MONICA HADDAD

Genesis Press, Inc.

INDIGO LOVE SPECTRUM

An imprint of Genesis Press, Inc.
Publishing Company

Genesis Press, Inc.
P.O. Box 101
Columbus, MS 39703

Copyright © 2011 Trisha Haddad and Monica Haddad

ISBN: 13 DIGIT : 978-1-58571-382-0
ISBN: 10 DIGIT : 1-58571-382-1
Manufactured in the United States of America

First Edition

Visit us at www.genesis-press.com
or call at 1-888-Indigo-1-4-0

DEDICATION

This book is dedicated to our parents, who always encouraged our creative endeavors and didn't actively discourage our gallivanting around the world (though we know you'd prefer we stay around Southern California).

Trisha also dedicates this book to her soul mate, Derek. For the real-life romance, *arigatou gozaimas!*

Monica also dedicates this book to her husband, Eddie. Thank you for marrying me before I became a famous writer and for the romantic inspiration to become one.

CHAPTER 1

Abigail Dennis ran her palm over the back of her neck, enjoying the air conditioned subway car. Holding the railing with her other hand, she stared at the advertisements that hung from the roof of the Meiko line train bound for Rokuban-cho station. She could rarely travel by subway without being stared at because of her dark complexion, the stares often accompanied by obvious pointing. But after living in Japan these past five years, she was used to it and avoided eye contact.

She scanned the omnipresent cell phone ad featuring a perky woman with the telephone headset, and then the Universal Studios Osaka ad of a roller coaster screaming through a violet sky.

Her eyes finally fell on the advertisement showing an ultra-blonde woman posing next to a Japanese high school student who had an English textbook casually tucked under his arm. A word bubble above them read "English World!"

English World, the folks that paid Abigail's salary. Or had done so until a week ago. They'd paid her right up until the coffers were empty, though the teachers had stopped getting paychecks nearly a month earlier.

Abigail was focusing on the English World ad when outside she caught sight of wavy golden hair in a sea of straight raven locks. The train pulled to a stop at Sakae station, and the golden mane swept toward the train, amidst the crowd of people.

"Excuse me," Abigail heard a sandpapery voice say from just outside the door. "Sorry. Excuse me."

Ah, the fellow was newly arrived. Not quite used to the close proximity of folks on the train. Not used to having to either push his way into the train or miss the train altogether. Abigail found herself hoping he'd make it on the train. She wanted to tell this newcomer to stop with the Western formalities and just push through the crowds.

She lost sight of his hair as the doors closed and turned back to the ads. Waiting for the train to move, she tugged at the Prussian blue jersey knit top that draped over her torso, skimming her curves and complementing her grey slacks. Suddenly she felt a tap on the shoulder.

"Excuse me. You look like a gal who understands English."

Abigail turned toward the tap, toward the sandpapery voice. There stood a tall, tanned, golden-waved Adonis. His eyes pierced her, a unique shade of light aqua. Only the crookedly awkward smile on his strong jaw seemed out of place.

Her voice caught in her throat.

The man smiled again. "English? Oh, I guess not. I'm sorry for bothering you."

Abigail shook off her surprise. "I speak English."

"Oh, fantastic." He sighed, his smile crooked at the right. "You stared at me for a second like everyone else here does."

"I wasn't expecting you."

"Expecting me?" The smile stayed put, and she noticed his eyes sweep from her short hair, down the length of her neck, and over her shoulders in one smooth motion.

Abigail touched the back of her neck again, a habit she had when she felt exposed. She certainly felt exposed now, as though his lips were touching the skin there. She hadn't been *expecting* to have her breath taken away by the sight of him.

"I mean, I wasn't expecting a question in English. Not today, anyway."

"And on other days?"

"I work at an English school, so yes, other days. Monday through Friday, and some Saturdays. But not today."

The train pulled into the next stop and the man glanced out the window. "Is this Hibino station?"

"It's pronounced *hee-bee-noh*, actually, rather than *hi-bine-oo*," she corrected him. "No, you still have four stops to go. And don't worry, by the end of your vacation, you'll have the hang of the Japanese train system."

"I'm not on vacation. I'm here to teach. Where do you teach?"

Abigail's stomach flipped. Surely Global Recruiting was not still promising jobs at English World . . . were they?

"I'm head administrator for the Nagoya branches of English World. Where are you teaching?"

"You must be Abigail Dennis. I'm with English World, too."

The crooked smile.

It didn't play well this time.

"There must be a mistake. I wasn't informed of a new teacher starting. Who was your recruiter?"

"Um." He reached into the back left pocket of his cargo shorts and emerged with a business card. "Hiroshi Taka-uh-takayama. I think he covers the Western U.S. He gave me a letter to give to you when I start on Monday. Sorry, but I don't have it right now; it's back at my room. Just moved in. He told me that there was a shortage of teachers, and if they didn't hire more they'd lose students."

You've got to be kidding me, Abigail thought. How should she explain the situation? Say that they needed teachers because the old ones were leaving in droves due to weeks without pay? Wait and call the recruiter for an explanation? Perhaps the investment deal that was supposed to save English World went through and paychecks would be coming any day now, as the head office in Tokyo had promised.

"What's your name?"

"London Crane. Is everything all right—"

The speakers announced the next stop, Higashi Betsuin. A wave of people moved out of the train. A wave of people moved into the train. Abigail looked out the window, trying to collect her thoughts. Her eyes focused instead on the faint reflection of London Crane running fingers through his hair, sweeping it back. When the train began moving again, she only replied, "Three more stops."

London ran his fingers through his hair again, pulling the waves back until they ricocheted into place. "Are you just uncomfortable because you're going to be my boss?"

"No, it isn't that."

"So," he started, and then hesitated. The crooked smile appeared again, "Does that mean there are no rules against fraternizing with the staff outside work hours?"

"Huh? Oh, well, no. It's different here. You said your recruiter was in the western U.S. office . . . Where in the States are you from?"

"Maui."

"That explains the sun-blond hair. You must be a surfer."

"Never got the hang of surfing, to be honest, but I am out on the water all the time. Where are you from?"

"San Diego, California."

"Then you know all about sun and surf."

"Suppose so. But I've been in Nagoya for five years already. It's home to me." The train stopped, unloaded and loaded, and continued on. "Two more stops."

"I know, Ms. Dennis, I can count. And I can tell something's bothering you."

Abigail arched an eyebrow.

"Really? You think you know me that well after speaking with me in a crowded train for a few minutes?"

"You didn't hide it very well that you weren't just surprised by my joining your school, you're also upset. You've made it clear that fraternizing isn't an issue. Made that quite clear." He winked at Abigail, who wondered if he'd gotten the wrong idea.

Abigail saw an open seat behind London. "Do you mind if I sit down? I've already been standing a while."

"Please," he replied, following her gaze and then motioning to the open seat. He turned and stood in front of her, not willing to let this go.

They slowed for Kanayama station. Most of the passengers exited, and very few entered. London sat down on the newly vacated seat next to Abigail.

"Next stop is yours, Mr. Crane."

"Call me London."

"Okay, London. I see you're not going to give this up. The thing is, English World is not doing well financially. You know how the global economy is right now. Japan is not immune. I run all of the Nagoya branches and haven't been paid in a week. Our teachers haven't been paid in a month. That's why there are so many open positions."

London's smile dropped. Abigail saw his eyes dim, and then a new spark flare up.

"What do you mean, the teachers haven't been paid?"

"They just haven't. I don't hand out the paychecks; they come from the head office in Tokyo, which keeps sending faxes asking everybody to hold on a little longer, saying they are getting things in order. Not many people can hold on that long. Not many people trust they'll ever get paid."

"And will they?"

"I think they will. I've been with English World for a good long time and they've always come through. I trust they are being honest, and that this is temporary."

"*Who* is being honest? Who are *they*?"

She stared at him, at his flaming eyes, his determined jaw. The crooked smile had been completely washed away. He'd posed a reasonable question. Who had she been so trusting of, after all?

"I don't know . . . the board of investors, the CEO, the president—"

"Don't you think you should know who it is you're trusting?"

"What does that mean?"

The chimes sounded and the train slowed.

"You ask me questions, but don't ask questions of your company? What kind of corporation gets away with treating their staff this way? And what kind of manager just lets them get away with it? Man, who knows? Maybe if you'd been more of a skeptic, you'd have seen this coming and been able to warn the teachers."

"You mean warn *you*? I didn't even know they were sending you. And this is your stop, by the way."

The train stopped and London stood up. "You didn't know I was coming. And yet these people you trust so much are hiring new employees knowing full well they won't get paid. Letting people move their entire life to a new country."

Abigail felt insulted but didn't have a ready answer. London shook his head, and she saw a hint of panic on his face. He'd just moved here. And now, for nothing.

London made his way to the door, and a feeling of regret flowed over her. She stood and followed him, grabbing his elbow before he stepped off the train. He whirled around.

"It's going to be fine. Don't panic. The school takes care of its staff."

"That's nice of you to say, Ms. Dennis, and I'm shocked, not panicked. I'll show up on Monday, but don't count on me for Tuesday."

The doors began to close and he hopped through, onto the platform. He turned and their eyes met as the train pulled away.

~~~

How could such a brief and seemingly inconsequential encounter have impacted her so deeply? Abigail lay on her side on the futon, staring out the low window of her bedroom. She had her window open and the fan on at the highest setting to battle the intense heat of the summer evening. However miserable the stifling humidity, the sound of the cicadas singing coupled with the fan working overtime brought a certain Zen to her evenings that none of the more tolerable seasons in Japan could match.

She then focused on the clock sitting atop the makeshift nightstand, one of her old suitcases turned on its side. Even after five years here, she'd not invested in nice furniture other than her futon, knowing at any time her visa might not be renewed and she'd have to go home. But tonight she wasn't worrying about her visa or going home, but about her many teachers who wanted to go home but didn't have the cash for airline tickets. She worried about the ones who wanted to stay in Japan and were desperately holding on, showing up at work and not getting paychecks, trusting English World because *she* trusted English World.

She'd been trying to sleep now for hours, and the sun would soon be rising. Abigail sat up and switched on the lamp. Until today, she'd been so sure things would improve. The company had been doing well financially for so many years, but now that the economy was weak it made sense that they'd need to reorganize and that maybe it would take a month or two. Not that it was acceptable, but Abigail could understand how it could happen.

And then London Crane from Maui showed up on a train with his crooked smile and good nature, his golden waves and his aqua eyes, and insisted that she question her assumptions. Who exactly did she trust? If a company were profitable for a time, why did she believe it was inherently honest? And if it were, why would it hire new teachers under false pretenses?

Had she made fools of the teachers she'd been meaning to reassure?

Abigail stood up and fanned herself. It was so damn humid. She'd taken a shower just before bed and now her skin felt sticky again. No matter how many summers she endured, she never quite got used to the humidity. She made her way to the sliding paper door and pushed it open, deciding that it was too close to morning to try to fall asleep and that she might as well get started on the day.

In the bathroom, she stared at her reflection for a long time. London Crane would be in the main office this morning, and he'd see her in this state. Great. She turned on the shower, determined to make the best of it.

∽⁇◌

By the time the sun rose, throwing orange streaks across the wood floor in her kitchen, Abigail was sitting at her tiny table in a light kimono-style robe, her short hair pulled off her forehead with a wide headband. One hand held a fan she'd bought on a weekend trip last fall to the island of Enoshima. Fanning herself with the hand-painted gold and black fan, she couldn't help remembering the long footbridge she'd taken to the mountain-island to see the famous Benten goddess statue. The island was dedicated to the goddess, who had supposedly made it rise up from the sea.

It had been a hefty climb up the steep staircase to see the delicate statue of the blue-haired goddess holding a lute. Instead of paying the thousand yen to take the island's fancy new escalator to the top, she'd climbed the stairs and saved her yen for shopping in town on the way back. The view of the statue and the purchase of the fan had been well worth the trip.

And now she watched the sun rise and fanned herself, trying to keep as cool as possible before she got to her air-conditioned school. She used her other hand to eat her tuna *onigiri*. When she first arrived, she'd had a hard time figuring out how to unpack these seaweed-covered balls of rice, but after mastering the fine art, she found them to be the perfect quick bite.

"At the check-in meeting this morning before school starts," she announced to the rising sun, "I'll explain that I'm not sure what's going on in Tokyo, that I'm going to be doing some investigating. Maybe they'll be angry, but at least I'll be honest. I've always been honest with them, even if my assumptions might turn out to have been wrong."

CHAPTER 2

When the train arrived at Hibino station, Abigail peered anxiously out the window onto the platform. The last thing she needed was more hounding to make her nervous before she met with the teachers this morning. When she didn't see the golden waves, she sighed in relief.

That is, until she reached the bustling hub of Nagoya station and stepped off the train.

His back was turned, but there was no denying it was him. He stood a head taller than anyone else in the vicinity. Golden waves cascaded to the nape of his neck, exposing just a sliver of sun-kissed skin between them and the collar of his crisp white shirt. She couldn't help admiring the wide back, the way his shirt tugged across his shoulders and the narrow waist that met navy blue slacks.

He was standing at a SunRUs, paying for whatever was on the counter, blocked from her view by his delicious body. She could have made a quick escape through the turnstiles but she admired him two seconds too long, and as she made a motion to go, he turned and saw her.

Their eyes locked.

It was clear that he was just as uncomfortable about running into her as she was about running into him. But there was no way Abigail was going to be the one to turn away rudely and head to the office, just to see him at a meeting in half an hour. She was his boss, after all, today at least, even if not on Tuesday.

He waited a moment, as though hoping she'd take the burden of rudeness, and when she didn't, he trudged toward her.

"Abigail Dennis," he said with a nod when he reached where she was standing. "Heading to the office, I presume."

"Yes. We have a check-in meeting every Monday before the teachers head to their respective schools. Classes start at ten. Do you know which school you'll be in?"

"The one next door to the office. The main school."

"For now, anyway."

The right side of London's mouth turned up into a crooked smile.

"Firing me already?"

"You plan to work Monday, but maybe not Tuesday. That's what you said on the train yesterday."

"Guess I did."

Abigail turned and made her way through the turnstiles, throwing over her shoulder, "I have to get to the office. Are you coming or will I just see you there?"

Silence. But Abigail didn't immediately concede by turning back to him. Seconds crawled by, and she slowed her pace in case he was following.

Finally, still without a reply, she turned around. "Are you coming or—"

But London was staring, captivated by a newspaper on display at a kiosk. He looked up.

"What is this about?" he asked, gesturing toward the newspaper.

"Mr. Crane, I really have got to get going." But then she sighed. "Well, if it's quick . . ."

She moved toward him and the kiosk. Before he could reply her eyes fell on the headline of the newspaper on display. Naturally, she focused first on the photo of the CEO, and then on the English words.

English World

She carefully read the Japanese characters that followed.

"What?" she muttered under her breath and picked up the paper. Abigail reached absently into her pocket for some yen, but before she could gather any, London handed the attendant the currency.

"Thanks," she said, looking up for the first time since reading the headline. His light aqua eyes weren't on her, though, but on the paper she was holding.

"What does it say?" he asked.

"English World CEO Missing." Abigail continued reading, vocalizing the highlights. "Mr. Inudori disappeared several days ago . . . The board just thought he'd taken time off . . ."

Abigail looked up at him and their eyes met, this time with a connection between them. "He didn't return."

"What?"

"They're thinking it's foul play," she explained.

"Foul play how? Like he ran off to a tropical island to save his own ass and let the company go under? Let the rest of you guys drown?"

Abigail skimmed further, turning to the inside page where the story continued. "Different theories . . . that's one of them—"

"What did I tell you about trusting those guys?"

"Hold up now. I said there were different theories. Some people think he's been kidnapped, or even murdered."

"Right. Nice cover. Who would have murdered the guy?"

"Maybe the investors have something to do with it. It says here the deal that was supposed to save the company fell through. His management has lost them a lot of money. It says some people think that a parent might have done something to him."

"His parents?"

"No, a parent of one of the students." Abigail looked up to explain. "The school's really expensive and they have to pay a year or more in advance, but there's so much pressure on families that a lot of people put their kids in a good *eikaiwa* even if it drains their finances."

"E-kai . . . what . . . ?"

"*Eikaiwa*. English language school. English World is one of the top schools. Or was. And very expensive. I guess I could see how someone might crack if they thought their money went down the drain."

"If he were murdered, it could also be a teacher."

"That's another theory. Some teachers are stuck here, you know. Don't have money for rent or food, or for a plane ticket home."

"That could lead someone to desperation."

"Exactly." Abigail thought of her teachers and checked her watch. "We have only twenty minutes until check-in. Better go. May I keep this newspaper?"

London followed her onto the street, where they turned right.

"Sure. I don't read those characters, er, letters . . ."

"*Kanji.*"

"Yeah, *kanji.*"

"Well, thanks for buying it."

After the news article, the tension between them was directed outside of the pair. As they walked, London felt the change first. Abigail's mind was occupied with what she'd say at the meeting.

He smiled crookedly. "I won't say I told you so, you know, about the execs being corrupt, because we don't know yet if the CEO is on the lam or if he's locked in someone's car trunk. But either way, this does make for an important twist in the school's future, don't you think?"

"I was thinking just that," she admitted. "I'd already planned to use our check-in to discuss the very real issues with the school's finances, even if I don't know all the details. This is just another thing I don't have any details about."

"What will you say?"

The pair turned left, where at the end of the street the blue and green English World logo hung perpendicular to the wall of the school's office.

"You'll be in the meeting, so you'll see then," she replied, realizing that she had no idea what she'd say now.

Abigail assumed by his change in gait that he took this as a brush-off. He straightened his back and turned his face forward rather than looking at her.

"Guess I will," he said as they reached the door. He held it for her, and she managed a smile for the receptionist.

"Saori, this is London Crane, a new teacher that Tokyo sent us. Can you get him settled in with paperwork before check-in? They said he'd be assigned to the main school."

Saori made eye contact with Abigail, who nodded, signaling she was just as confused by the new addition. Along with the rest of the Japanese staff, Saori hadn't been paid in two months, apparently because headquarters knew that the Japanese staff would suffer through nonpayment with less protest than the foreign staff.

Then, with a sympathetic smile toward London, Abigail turned on her heels and made her way to her office to figure out in fifteen minutes what she could say to her staff that would be both honest and relevant, with what little she knew about the situation in which they found themselves.

❧

Abigail fought the urge to touch the back of her neck, despite feeling uneasy and exposed, and managed a smile for the group. Gazing out at the faces in the room that in turn focused on her, she estimated a little over twenty people had showed up. Just six months ago there had been nearly sixty teachers in this meeting to hear the latest school news and get lesson plans for the week. For the past two months fewer and fewer teachers showed up for the Monday meetings, and the large room now looked almost empty.

This meeting would be different.

"Thank you for coming," she started, instantly and unintentionally making eye contact with London Crane. She pulled her gaze away and scanned the room purpose-fully, making eye contact with a teacher here and there for emphasis.

"I really mean that. Thank you. As I see it, we have two elephants in the room here, and let's get right to them. One is the arrival of a new teacher. Everyone, this is London Crane from the U.S."

She smiled at London, an unspoken apology for making him the brief center of attention. A din rose in the crowd.

"Global Recruiting sent him here without informing me. I met him on the train this weekend. His unan-nounced arrival has drawn my attention to the fact that Tokyo has not been as honest with me as I'd thought they were. For that, folks, I am so sorry. I hope you believe that I've been acting in good faith each and every time I told you that English World had been good to me and that I trusted them."

All eyes were intent on her.

"The second and more concerning elephant in the room is this." She held up the newspaper that London had bought her.

"You may or may not have seen this article this morning. I understand not everyone can read *kanji*, so I'll paraphrase. Our CEO is missing."

Voices rose all at once, but no actual words were distinguishable. When Abigail held her hand up to silence them, it only cut the noise level in half.

"No one knows where he is. I'm afraid that some think he's been kidnapped or that he is dead. Others," she looked again to London, "think he's run off with his money so that he can't be blamed for what is happening with the school. I don't know which it is. The police don't know. The board doesn't know.

"This leaves us in an awkward situation. I fully appreciate the fact that you've continued working with the hope of being paid any day now. So have I. And now I don't know if we can hold on to that hope. At least, not to the hope that things will get better soon. I'm guessing the focus will be on finding Mr. Inudori, rather than on paying us."

At the front of the room, a young man raised his hand. Abigail nodded at him.

"You have a question, Matt?"

"This might sound trivial," he said quietly, "but if you're not getting paid, will you still be providing rice, ramen and tea in the lounge in case we can't afford food?"

A woman barely twenty years old spoke up.

"Yeah, I know it seems like a selfish question, but I was thinking the same thing. I can't buy food right now, and I've been kind of relying on that."

"But if Miss Dennis isn't getting paid either," an Australian woman replied, "it isn't fair for us to expect it."

London was listening to the conversation and turned to the Canadian standing next to him. Abigail could barely hear him ask, "She pays for food for you guys?"

"Since they stopped paying us she's been buying food to have available for those of us who are struggling, or whose parents aren't wiring them cash."

London looked back at Abigail, a deeply interested look on his face.

A mental picture of her bank account flashed in Abigail's mind. Thankfully she'd saved well over the years, but between supplying food for the teachers and not getting a paycheck, her savings were rapidly dwindling.

"I'll be providing food long as I have money in my savings account. And please don't worry about my finances; they are mine to worry about.

"But this does bring me to another point. How many of you are in apartments owned by English World?"

Three-quarters of the teachers raised their hands.

"Good. If you haven't already, go online to the company website and switch your rent so that it comes out of your paychecks. That way, you'll be essentially living there for free as long as you are working for free. But remember that when they start paying us again, rent will come out of the checks again, including back rent coming out of back pay. So this isn't a free ride."

From the looks on the teachers' faces, this was not news to many of them.

"And I would ask personally, and not as your boss, that those of you who are lucky enough to have company housing consider offering housing to your colleagues who don't. It would help a fellow teacher out . . . and in turn help you out if it means they continue coming to work so you don't have to pick up the slack. Any questions about that?"

Only the golden-waved American spoke up now, and though he was still feisty, he'd softened in Abigail's opinion from their first encounter on the train.

"This may have been answered in previous meetings, and if so, excuse me. But why are any of you still here? Why not all walk out? Including you, Miss Dennis?"

Abigail opened her mouth to speak, but to her surprise her staff spoke first.

"Our kids still need us."

"Their parents have paid up to two years in advance."

"A lot of families struggle to send their kids here, and they couldn't pay even more to enroll them elsewhere at such short notice."

"Exams are coming soon and it wouldn't be right to leave them out in the cold."

"It isn't our students' fault the company's not paying us."

Abigail swelled with pride. They got it. Her eyes moistened as she thought of the warm hearts in the room, and it was hard for her to interrupt them, but she did her duty.

"That is exactly why, Mr. Crane. I know you've not started here yet, haven't met any of the students, and don't know the drill. You may be used to other companies where the staff is just there to make money. But your colleagues here have articulated it correctly. Teaching is more than a job. It is kind of a calling. And these fine folks are staying as long as they can for the same reason I am. The students and their families."

❧

At the end of the day, London was waiting for her outside.

"Miss Dennis!" he called when she opened the door. Over the hubbub of the businessmen heading home from their offices, his sandpapery voice was clear.

She stopped in her tracks, startled at his sudden proximity. The door swung closed behind her.

"Sorry to startle you, Miss Dennis. Thought you might not have seen me and I wanted to catch you before you left for the train."

Abigail looked politely at him, avoiding his aqua eyes. To look into his eyes would be to offer him a glance into hers. And if he were to look in her eyes, he'd surely see a mix of anxiety and lust.

"Hello, Mr. Crane. Nice to see you again. I must get to the station before my train leaves, so if you'll excuse me—"

"Let me walk you to the station."

"I suppose that would be all right."

They started down the street, and she asked, "How was your first day teaching English in Japan?"

"It went well. The students sure do want to learn, don't they? I can see how it's easy to get attached to them."

Abigail smiled and allowed her eyes to meet his just briefly. It was enough. He smiled his crooked smile, and his aqua eyes lit up. He had seen what she'd wanted so desperately to hide.

London cleared his throat as they turned right and headed down the street. "Anyway, like I said before, I'm glad I was able to catch you on your way out. I want to apologize."

"For what?" she asked, keeping her eyes forward and walking at a brisk pace. If she missed the train, there would be another one within fifteen minutes. But what might he say in those fifteen minutes that would keep her up all night again?

"I'm sure you know what, but it wouldn't be much of an apology if I left it at that." London laughed to himself before continuing. "I'm sorry for what I said on the train yesterday. I had no right to make the assumptions I did without even knowing you and . . . damn, I don't even remember exactly what I said. I just know the emotion I had behind it, and when you looked at me through the window as the train pulled away, I thought I might have been kind of a jerk. And hearing your staff talk about you today, I realize I'd judged you too quickly."

Abigail smiled inwardly. She'd worried all night about the things he'd said, and now he couldn't even recall what they were. She'd acted as though he had some divine revelation for her, and he'd just been bitching.

"You didn't seem to think you'd been wrong when we ran into each other this morning." She couldn't hide the sarcasm.

"I didn't say I thought I was wrong, just that I'd been a jerk. I only realized I'd been wrong this morning in the meeting."

"Never knew I was such a persuasive orator."

"Look, I'm apologizing, which means I know I was wrong. You don't have to reiterate that." London smiled then, and his face softened. "Unless it will help you forgive me."

They made a right, into the station. Abigail dug through her bag, searching for her subway pass as the two maneuvered through the maze of stairs and businessmen. When they reached the turnstiles, Abigail swiped her pass and walked through in one smooth motion. Behind her, an alarm sounded and the gates shut London out of the subway platform. London bowed with embarrassment to the irritated Japanese businessmen behind him and stood to the side. Stifling giggles, Abigail stopped to wait for him on the other side of the railing.

"Do you have a subway pass?" she asked, holding hers up.

"Yeah, but it wouldn't go through. Am I doing it wrong?"

Abigail watched him try again, and reached over to flip the card when he put it in backwards.

"I forgive you, and sorry about the sarcasm," she continued when he'd successfully come through the turnstile. "I didn't get a lot of sleep last night, thanks to you."

"Our meeting kept you up?"

"What you *said* kept me up," she quickly corrected him. But heat rose in her cheeks. How cocky he was! But a guy that looked like that must have grown up with admiring women all around him. And now he'd be offended that she wasn't partaking in his playful flirting.

Instead, he caught her eyes with his and stared intently.

"Then it must have resonated."

"It did."

"Maybe I'll revise my apology. I'm sorry for having been so attacking. I should have said . . . whatever I said . . . in a more diplomatic way."

Finally Abigail smiled, and touched him tentatively on the forearm. It was a go-to gesture she used regularly with her teachers. Casual but reserved. Professional, but with a dash of *I-understand-and-care*.

But London's arm was firm, ropes of muscles easily discernible under the thin fabric of his shirt. And he held her gaze with as much intensity as before. Though she'd meant the gesture to be professional, the electric currents that flowed between her fingertips and his forearm were anything but.

She withdrew her hand and looked to the platform as a few notes of music chimed the train's approach.

London said suddenly, "Well, I sure am ready to find a good place to get some food."

"If you haven't tried *omurice* yet, its Spanish-style rice with cooked egg over it, and different fixings. There's a good place a few floors up called Molette. Try the dish with barbeque sauce. It's surprisingly good."

London stared at her as though he were shocked she couldn't discern what he was building up to. Finally, as the train pulled to a stop, he translated for her.

"Miss Dennis," he said finally, "I'd like to treat you to dinner . . . as part of my apology."

"My train's just arrived," she said before she even acknowledged the words coming out of her mouth, motioning to the train pulling up to a stop. "And like I said, I didn't sleep much last night and should get home."

"Then tomorrow night."

"Well, I—"

"Or the next," he joked, "or the next."

London smiled crookedly, and Abigail couldn't help laughing at his false desperation. "London, don't think you need to buy me a meal for me to accept your apology! I said you were forgiven."

"I know . . ."

The train stopped and two people exited while a flood moved toward it, dragging Abigail firmly toward the doors.

"Glad you know," she called to him, laughing as she was carried inside.

"It was just an excuse to take you out!" he called back, his laugh as rough as his voice.

The door closed before she could acknowledge his words and, surrounded by dark suits, she could see the platform no longer.

CHAPTER 3

Teachers wouldn't be expected for classes until ten; only Abigail and the office receptionist arrived at eight. So Abigail was surprised to hear the door chime at eight-fifteen. She was certain that it would be another teacher coming in to say he or she was going home. She couldn't blame them, but it didn't make scheduling classes any easier, either.

She remained still, but the receptionist did not page her, and no one entered her office. After a muffled conversation in low voices, she heard the chime again.

Her curiosity overcame her, and she poked her head out the door. "Saori," she called out. "Who just came and left?"

She heard a giggle, before the receptionist replied, "Someone wanting to know if you preferred tea or coffee."

"Who was it?" Abigail asked, heading to the front desk.

"The new teacher. The one that looks like a Hollywood star."

"London Crane. Interesting."

"That's what I thought, also."

"He's going to bring me a drink?"

"Perhaps. He did not say. I thought it was interesting that he asked about you. Is there something going on between you and Mr. Crane?"

Abigail looked toward the front door. "No. But he did kind of insult me when we first met on the train, and yesterday he apologized."

"What did he say to insult you?"

"Never mind that . . . it isn't relevant."

"So you're thinking he's trying to earn your forgiveness with a drink?"

"He's already tried to bribe me with dinner. Have you talked much to him? Before just now, I mean?"

"I gave him the information for starting the job. And I tried to talk to him more in the afternoon, but he said he had to be somewhere. Now I am thinking it was a dinner date with you. It sounds as if you have finally found someone you are interested in dating." She smiled.

"I didn't take him up on his offer. I was really tired and anxious to get home. And besides, I understand he was upset at having moved here under false pretenses . . . he doesn't need to buy me food to make me forgive him. I mean, we're adults, and I'm not one to hold a grudge."

Saori's jaw had dropped slightly, and now she insisted, "How do you turn away a man like that, Abigail? Don't you find him attractive?"

"I was tired. Simple as that. Yes, he's good looking; anyone can see that. But is that reason enough for me to change my plans because he wants to have dinner?"

Saori smirked, and Abigail knew it meant *she'd* change her plans for a guy like that. Abigail looked toward the door again.

"Geez, is he bringing me tea or what?"

"Are you anxious for some tea, or are you anxious to see him?"

"I'm anxious to see if he's going to bring me some tea. I actually have half a cup of tea still in my office."

She tapped on Saori's desk twice, and with a sigh said, "Well, I'm going to get back to it. If he shows up, send him on back."

He didn't show. Abigail finished the rest of her tea and avoided making another cup in case. But now that it was nearly ten he'd be in class, and she had to make her way to the class she'd taken over from a departed teacher.

Her first class was always Abigail's favorite of the day. The company had recently launched a new lesson titled "Talk About" to help boost lesson sales to current students who wanted time away from the books. It was a time to talk candidly in English about whatever topic came up. She peeked through the window of the classroom and saw eight adult students talking amongst themselves in Japanese, waiting for her arrival. She caught pieces of their conversation through the window.

"Do you think a teacher will come?"

"I've already paid for two years."

"The CEO is missing."

She straightened her skirt and jacket and picked up a copy of *Japan Times*, an English-language newspaper, for some current event topics and turned the doorknob.

As soon as she walked in, everyone greeted her with thanks and immediately asked if she or the other teachers had been paid yet. In the past, she had avoided the question so as not to get English World in any more trouble than it already was, but now that the school was headline news, there was no denying it. She answered the questions as honestly as possible, but as soon as there was a break in questions, she turned the discussion to the topic she had chosen for the class.

"I read in the newspaper today that Japanese high school students are not performing well on international standardized testing. Why do you think this is?"

The class became quiet and she regretted the topic, thinking that the level she chose was too high for these students. One student picked up his Japanese-English dictionary and started searching frantically, while others fanned themselves with advertisement fans for the "pay-by-the-hour" love hotel down the street, trying hard not to make eye contact. One student, Atsushi, was slinking in the corner with his arms crossed.

Atsushi's company had been paying for him to attend English World for four years, and it had worked. He had reached the highest level given to students attending English World and no longer attended regular lessons. He still attended "Talk About" lessons, though no teacher in the Nagoya schools really knew why. He had a difficult and surly personality and rarely "talked about" anything. The common theory amongst the teachers was that Atsushi wanted to keep his English fresh to help tutor his son, who was coming up on exams. Abigail, however, thought he seemed to rather enjoy sitting in the corner scoffing at his classmates' responses.

Abigail started to rephrase the question, but Atsushi suddenly spoke up, focusing intently on Abigail.

"Maybe it's because parents give millions of yen to big schools and then no teachers come to the lessons."

Immediately the conversation took off.

Students defended the teachers, insisting that it was not the teachers' fault that the school was not paying them. They said that the classes at English World were top-notch, and that the high school students there had a better chance of passing exams than if they hadn't invested in English World.

Abigail recognized this argument as coming directly from an advertising campaign several years back.

More students with passing scores. Invest in your child. Invest in English World.

English errors flew around the room with the heated argument, but Abigail could not calm the students down long enough to correct them. So much for investing in English World.

When the bell signaling the end of class rang, the class granted her thirty seconds of attention to say their farewells before continuing their argument in Japanese.

She walked briskly to her office to get the materials for her next lesson. Still no tea. She checked the roster for her next five lessons, all overbooked. She missed the days when the office was bustling with teachers complaining about students and talking about the previous night's social escapades. Now only she and Saori were in the office, and Saori was always busy with angry parents of students who couldn't schedule their lessons.

The bell rang for the next class and she went on with her day. Vocabulary. Listen and Repeat. Comprehension. Homework help. It was the drill that all English World teachers knew by heart. It escaped being monotonous because of the clever students making jokes and inter-acting with the foreign teachers in a way that would not have been tolerated in their regular schools.

Regardless of the state of English World, the corpora-tion, Abigail took pride in the work she and her staff were doing day to day. Not only that, but she knew she wasn't only teaching English, but also exposing the next genera-tion of Japanese men and women to new social norms and people. Her students knew her as an intelligent, caring human being, not an oddity to gawk at on the subway.

When the school day was over, Abigail headed back to her office for a quick check of email and voicemail before heading home. As she stood outside the door to her office, she wondered if there would be a cup of cold tea sitting on her desk, perhaps with a note of apology. Or a note informing her that the blond with the aqua eyes had headed back to Maui after all.

She slid the door open.

On her desk sat a black and red tray with a small, delicate black tea kettle next to two perfect tea cups and saucers. She picked up the kettle and rotated it until vibrant red *kanji* came into view.

"Trust," she translated aloud. She looked at the desk again, but there was no note.

No sooner had she set the kettle back on the tray than she heard from behind her, "How about some tea then?"

She whirled around and there he was, holding two tea bags and a pitcher of steaming water.

"Did you leave this here, London?"

"It's a gift. The character reads TRUST. That's what the guy selling it to me said, anyhow."

"He was telling the truth," was all she could mutter.

"Grab it and come up to the roof with me and let's have some tea."

London didn't wait for a response. He turned on his heels and headed toward the stairs that led to the roof.

Abigail stood motionless for a moment, but he wasn't standing there any longer; if she were to argue, to whom would she direct her argument? So she gathered up the tray and followed him to the stairs and up onto the roof.

She hadn't been up here for at least six months, being so consumed with the work that waited for her under the roof. As she came through the door and into the air, however, the light breeze kissed her cheeks and neck and the late afternoon light scattered over the gravel rooftop.

"I forgot how nice it was up here," she started, lowering herself to a sitting position next to London, who was already sprawled out on a blanket. "What made you think to come up here?"

"I saw the sign on the door saying it was the stairs to the roof. And I tested the door and realized it wasn't locked."

London filled the kettle with the hot water in his pitcher and pulled the cups toward himself. "I'll get this set up."

"I can do it."

"Just enjoy the view, Abigail. Let me take care of this."

Abigail stretched her legs out in front of her and leaned back on her hands. She watched as he undid the wrist buttons and rolled up the sleeves on his pale canary shirt, exposing tanned forearms. Fine blond hair flecked his arms, and even as he maneuvered the tea cups and kettle, she could see the muscles below the skin flex.

He slid a cup toward her, careful to turn it so the string on the tea bag was close to her to ease its removal.

"When I saw this tea set, I thought it was perfect for you. I checked with Saori to be sure you drank tea before I bought it."

"You said I was wrong to trust."

"Turns out you just trusted the wrong people. But *surrounding* you is trust. You trust your staff to make the right choices for themselves and help one another if they can. Your staff trusts that you have their best interests in mind. And I," he added with a twinkle in his aqua eyes, "trust you've forgiven me for misjudging you."

Abigail removed the tea bag and set it on the saucer. "I told you I forgave you. You didn't have to buy me anything."

She wanted to add that if he were smart he'd save his money, because there was no way of knowing now when he'd be paid.

"I'm not trying to bribe you," he argued with a gentleness that made her believe he was telling the truth. "I'm very impressed with the relationship you have with your staff, and when I saw this I thought it was meant for you."

He removed the tea bag from his cup and held it up. "To trust," he announced.

Abigail smiled and raised her own glass before taking a sip. "Good job with the tea, London. It's delicious. And thank you for the gift. It is very . . . sweet."

She cast her eyes at her cup with the final word, shy to be saying it. Maybe it was the delicious, warm tea. Maybe it was the bronze sun quietly dipping into the horizon before her eyes. But after five years of little interest in dating—especially with all the Japanese men who now and then asked her for sex, something she later found out black women in Japan often dealt with—she found herself curious about London. And even interested.

They sat in silence for a few moments, each sipping their tea. Finally she spoke again. "What did you do back in Hawaii? Were you a teacher?"

"No, I . . ." he paused, seeming to be searching for the right words before saying, ". . . worked in hospitality."

"Hospitality? Like a hotel or a restaurant or something like that?"

"Yeah, exactly. At a hotel in Kaanapali. Managed the place, but what I really liked was leading the kayak tours. You know, taking guests kayaking to see sea turtles, the reef, stuff like that."

Abigail glanced at his wide shoulders and now recognized the source of their definition and strength. "Kayaking! What a life to live!"

"No kidding. The sun on your back and ocean spray on your face. I'll never say it wasn't quite a place to live and work. Even with rude guests once in a while, most people were decent, and I always enjoyed hearing their stories. Where they lived, how they chose to vacation in Maui, their hopes and goals."

"So why did you leave?"

"You mean to come here to work at a job without pay?"

"You obviously didn't know that. But why did you leave at all? If you wanted to see Japan, you could have always just vacationed here."

"I've visited Japan before."

London took another sip of his tea and set it down beside him. He leaned back on his elbows, sighed, and watched the bronze sun.

"The hotel I worked at, well, I suppose you could say it's in the family. And with the economy as it is, people don't book vacations to the tropics after they've been laid off or lost their homes. So things tightened up at the hotel, and we naturally needed to make some cuts."

"Your family laid you off?" she asked, removing her light jacket and setting it to the side. Though it was evening, it was too warm to have on any layers over her sleeveless shell without air conditioning.

"Not exactly, but I was one of two kayak tour guides. The other one had a wife and kids to take care of, and I didn't want him to be laid off. I didn't need the job, *per se,* and he did. It was easy for me to get up and go anywhere, something he couldn't do. So I decided to try something completely different from anything I'd ever done before."

Abigail examined the length of his legs, which were stretched out before him. He didn't seem at all concerned that his chocolate-colored slacks would get dirty or torn on the gravelly rooftop where the blanket ended. Before she could respond, he kicked off his shoes and leaned forward to pull off his socks.

Suddenly, he stopped to look at her.

"You don't mind, do you?"

"No, please go ahead."

"Thanks. I'm not used to wearing shoes and socks all day." He rolled up his slacks, and the sun hitting the tanned skin on his ankles made the bone structure glow.

Abigail knew she shouldn't have been surprised at the fact that English World had sent her a teacher with no teaching experience. Beggars couldn't be choosy. But the standards certainly had dropped.

"It was a good thing of you to do," Abigail finally replied.

"I know I should be like, 'Aw, it was nothing,'" London said and threw a casual and crooked smile over to her. "But it was a hard decision to leave my hotel and I have to admit I feel good about making it. It's too early to say I feel good about the decision to come here, but I can say I feel good that I took a chance. Do you ever feel that way about things? Like it was the right thing to do, so you shouldn't necessarily feel cocky about it, but you do anyway?"

Abigail thought about it a moment.

"I guess I do. Never thought about it. But, for example, buying food for my teachers. It isn't the most financially savvy thing to do right now, but it does seem to be the right thing to do. And I admit that I feel good about doing it."

Abigail smiled at her own candid reply. The sun touched the horizon and glowed intensely.

"I'm glad you came up here with me, Abigail. I had a feeling it would be a good place to be with you."

"Why?"

"The way you say that sounds less confident than the woman I've sensed you to be."

"I didn't mean it that way. I'm not one of those self-loathing women. But why me, why you, why now and here?"

London leaned closer to her, and Abigail took another sip of tea to steady her nerves. Anyone else and it would have been just another conversation. But

London's waves swayed in the breeze, catching glimmers of sunlight on the edges. Every once in a while a curl would fall over his aqua eyes.

"Because I admire the choices you make and how you treat those around you."

He didn't add a thing about physical attraction, but she watched as his eyes traced her neck, her bare shoulders, and her arms. He didn't linger, but before bringing his gaze back to her face, he skimmed her hips against the blanket.

Her heart leapt into her throat. It was not a lewd look in the slightest, but she imagined his hands grasping her hips, drawing her up, pressing her body against his chest.

"Thank you," she choked out, immediately looking away.

"Good view, isn't it?"

"Y—yes. The sun is nearly down."

"And what are your plans after sunset?"

Regaining her composure, Abigail looked at him. She fought the urge to answer honestly and say she would head home for dinner of leftover *udon* noodles and *mochi,* and then to bed with the newest Eliza Tahan bestseller, *The Sands of Botswana.*

"Not sure yet," she lied coyly. "The evening could go in any direction."

"Was our tea and sunset a good start?"

"I'd say so."

"Then stay a while, Abigail. I can boil some more water downstairs and grab a couple more bags of tea."

"I should probably leave it at one cup for me, so I can sleep tonight."

London took her empty cup and placed it next to his on the tray before scooting closer to her, their shoulders grazing. "Then let's just stay. Get to know one another."

"And what do you mean by that?"

Without a hint of tentativeness, London wrapped his arm around her shoulders.

"Talk. And watch the stars come out."

She leaned into him and gazed up at the violet sky.

CHAPTER 4

She'd been staring at the email draft for the last ten minutes, reading and re-reading what she'd written the day before. She was emailing one of her counterparts, Savannah Thompson, the administrative head of the Osaka branch of English World and a good friend. The purpose was to ask how she was managing the situation in her schools. If English World wasn't going to give them information or guidance, perhaps the pair could brainstorm. They might even be able to come up with some "best practices" to share with their counterparts nationwide.

As complex a topic as it was, the email wasn't the problem. She couldn't focus. Her eyes skimmed the words on the screen but only one word repeated in her mind.

London.

Their evening on the roof hadn't been the most adventurous thing she'd done in Japan by a long shot. Maybe not even the most fun. But it resonated with her like no experience had in the recent past. It had been a time to pause and experience. Experience the taste of the warm sweet tea on her tongue, the glow of the sun as it hit the horizon, the geometric shapes of the buildings in silhouette, the pinpoints of light appearing as the sky faded from dusky violet to midnight blue to obsidian.

And to experience the weight of London's arm over her shoulder, the heat of his skin against hers. What had he meant by the gesture?

More importantly, what had she meant by leaning into him, resting her head against his firm chest? He'd seemed surprised by her willingness, but soon settled his chin on the top of her head.

She re-read the email draft aloud.

Dear Savannah,
You've certainly heard the news about Mr. Inudori. I've received no response from headquarters regarding the status of our staff's pay or the future of the school. I doubt you have, either, or you would have let me know. I propose we take this on ourselves.

We should have a discussion and maybe a meeting to brainstorm the next steps for our staff and local schools. I'm sure you're in the same boat as I am: not enough staff to teach the students, upset students and parents as we approach exam time, and a staff that can last only so long without pay.

That was all she had, and she was anxious to get on to something else.

Abigail took a deep breath, knowing she needed to finish this now or she'd never get to it. She spoke aloud as she wrote.

Can we plan a call to talk about this? I know you must be as busy as I am. But any time we can squeeze in will be helpful, I think.

Best wishes,
Abigail

She leaned back for a moment before deleting the closing and instead typing *Talk to you soon*, followed by her first name. She pressed SEND before she could change her mind.

Abigail stood up and stretched her arms over her head. The thought of calling London crossed her mind, but she had promised one of her teachers that she'd show up at Tsurumai Park to support his busking.

One of her ever-optimistic Australian teachers, John, had just been evicted from his apartment and was hoping to get some sympathy—and yen—by playing his guitar in the park outside his apartment complex. He wasn't expecting Abigail and his fellow teachers to pony up some yen, but he did want a little support.

She opened the tall locker next to her desk and reached in for her purse. Looking in the mirror that hung on the door, she adjusted her headband. Deep in her eyes, she noticed something new. Was it passion? No, she'd been passionate about her work and about her surroundings long before now.

No . . . it was a flirtation that hadn't been there before. She smiled at her flirty reflection.

"Well, Abigail, we certainly do surprise ourselves, don't we?"

∞

The sun was setting as Abigail arrived at Tsurumai station. After being carried away with the rush hour crowd, she emerged in the park surrounded by green. As she stopped for a moment to take it in, she heard a thoughtful voice behind her.

"The humidity is miserable, but when you realize it creates landscape like this, you can't entirely hate it."

Abigail recognized the accent and timbre immediately. She turned toward her friend, who spotted her and finished up the cell phone call she was in the midst of.

"Abby!" she cried when she had shut the flip phone.

"Cheryl! I didn't know you were coming!"

The two women hugged.

Abigail and Cheryl had arrived on the same train to Nagoya five years ago, and had gravitated toward each other when they realized they were reading the same *Living in Japan* instructional book. Throughout their five years in Japan, they'd remained close, even though Cheryl was stationed outside of Nagoya in the suburbs.

There was silence after the embrace as the two linked arms and looked over the park glowing warmly in the light from the sunset.

"I'm going to miss it," Cheryl whispered to herself.

Abigail glanced over at her friend in surprise. Cheryl's strong facial features contradicted her delicate frame. One of her students had once told Cheryl she had an "oriental mask", and, as much fun as she had had with the phrase, it was remarkably true.

Cheryl had been born in Hong Kong but raised in Canada, where she became one of most independent women Abigail knew. In Japan, she was constantly mistaken for a Japanese woman, and she tended to cause more of a reaction when she reprimanded a pervert on the train than Abigail did. It was as though onlookers expected such behavior from a black woman, but not a Japanese woman.

"Miss? What do you mean you'll miss this?" Even as Abigail asked, she knew the answer, and dreaded it.

Cheryl broke her gaze and shook her head, returning to reality.

"My savings are gone. I just maxed out my credit card buying a ticket back home. I'm leaving tomorrow night."

"When did you book your flight?"

"This morning. A last-minute travel deal. All I could afford, and I wasn't sure I could afford that. Luckily, I'll be on Singapore Airlines, though. If it had been an American airline they'd probably charge me for luggage. I just don't have the money for that."

"Will you be moving back in with your folks?"

"No, some friends. For now. Got to find a job at home, and then I'll figure something out."

"I'm really sorry to have you go, Cheryl. Not to make you feel bad, but I will miss you."

"Me, too." Her eyes misted, but she countered it with a light smile. "John better be a damn good guitar player if I'm spending my last night here listening to him *busk*!"

Abigail laughed half-heartedly and the two women made their way toward the faint guitar melody coming from the gazebo in the center of the park.

News like this was nothing new to Abigail, especially lately, but Cheryl's sudden departure made her feel instantly lonely. Cheryl and Abigail were the last ones remaining from the group of teachers that they came over with.

In the past, she'd always loved how life was so fleeting within the community of *gaijin*—foreigners—because it made every moment and memory that much more precious. However, now she found herself longing for something firm to hold onto during all this turmoil.

The faint guitar music rose to a crescendo and John's cello-esque voice rang out a line from the chorus of Leonard Cohen's "Hallelujah." If Abigail didn't know him any better, she'd have assumed he found himself in the depths of despair. But sad as the music sounded, sad as the lyrics were, it was all the song and not the singer. Not this singer.

The guitar, like everything else in Japan, seemed dwarfed by John's tall, hulking frame. He was the epitome of the stereotypical square-shouldered Australian Abigail always pictured when she thought about crocodile hunters and rugby players. He always surprised her with his warmth and general bohemian nature.

John smiled at Abigail and Cheryl's arrival, but they could instantly tell by the empty guitar case and the fact that only a smattering of equally poor foreigners mulled about that the evening had yet to be fruitful.

After an improvised final chord progression, John put his guitar down to greet them. Abigail looked at his empty guitar case and translated the *kanji* sign.

"Will teach English for food. Cute."

John laughed, "Back at home, I would have gotten at least a few dollars for being clever, but Japanese people seem too scared to even stop to read it. I heard one man

47

tell another in Japanese that a teacher murdered Inudori. Then they both eyed me like I could've done it."

"And that's without even knowing about your tendency to try extreme activities! Anyway, have you found a new apartment? Did you ask Matt if you could crash at his company apartment for a while?"

"I'll be couch-surfing all next week. I have a brilliant plan after that."

"Oh, and what is this brilliant plan of yours?" Cheryl pressed, obviously intrigued. Abigail couldn't immediately discern if Cheryl was trying to find out if it were a plan she might be able to use instead of going home . . . or if Cheryl still harbored a secret crush on their Australian colleague.

Abigail had to admit that John tended to come up with the most unique schemes. One spring, he had hitch-hiked north following the cherry blossoms all the way up to Hokkaido. That time, as usual, the teachers had teased that it would never work and when he returned triumphant, they all felt a little sorry they hadn't taken the chance and gone along with him.

John stood up proudly, stretching his arms behind him.

"Korea's hiring teachers from Japan left and right, and they pay for your housing and health insurance completely. I'm going to hitchhike down to Hakata. One of the guys I met down there last spring works the ferries that go to Busan. He said he could probably sneak me on for free. And then, hopefully, I'll get a job."

"Why don't you just apply online? From what I hear, they reply pretty quick. I'm sure you could stay with someone until then."

"Nah, this is more fun. Might as well enjoy my last little while in Japan."

"You have more guts than I do," Cheryl said, obviously impressed, and obviously still crushing.

"Speaking of which, Abigail, I'll need to resign next Friday before the holiday, but I promise I'll keep coming in every day until then. Sorry, I know it's tough for you and the students, but I just can't afford it anymore."

"I understand completely. It sounds like quite an adventure. And I appreciate that you stayed for as long as you did. If English World ever ends up paying us, I'll make sure you get paid."

He removed his already loosened tie. He had obviously come here straight from work. The image of London's broad shoulders and cascading blond waves filled Abigail's mind as she remembered that the two men worked at the same branch.

John went back to the gazebo steps, strumming aimlessly on his guitar and laughing with Cheryl. Abigail took a seat next to them.

"Did anyone else show up at your branch today?" Cheryl asked him. "There were only two teachers at my branch; it was tough. I'm really looking forward to the *O-bon* holiday for a break."

"Yeah," John replied. "Actually, everyone scheduled came in today! Can you believe it? Even that new Hawaiian guy came—the high school girls love him! He's with the others getting some drinks from the convenience store."

Abigail's heartbeat quickened as she remembered his silhouette against the sunset on the school rooftop.

"Nice." Cheryl smiled "Typical bohemians! They don't have enough money for food and housing, but they have enough for alcohol!"

"Alcohol is cheaper than rent," John countered. Then he started singing as he modulated to an appropriate key, "*Viva la vie boheme!*"

The sun had set and the Christmas lights lining the gazebo came on, giving the night a starlit feeling despite the city lights dimming the actual stars.

On the other side of the park, there was a squeal and then an explosion in the sky, followed by an uproar of laughter. The source of such enjoyment came from a group of the "loud, rude *gaijin*" the older students, such as Atsushi, liked to complain about. It was obvious that they had already started drinking on their walk over.

"We come bearing gifts," one of the younger guys shouted across the park as they approached.

Abigail scanned the group, and even in the dim light from the gazebo she could make out London's towering frame and bright, crooked smile. He'd distanced himself from the rowdier younger guys, almost like an older brother waiting to step in if things got out of hand.

She stood up and instantly their eyes met. Everything else went faint.

Suddenly she felt something icy on the back of her neck. She spun around to find Cheryl with her favorite convenience store canned cocktail—lychee flavor—pressed to her skin.

By the time she turned back around, London was only inches away. His arm enveloped her shoulders.

"This is too beautiful," he told her, smiling as he took a sip from his canned cocktail.

His sandpapery voice and musky scent made the ground under Abigail sway.

"It sure is."

She regained her composure, popped open her lychee cocktail and raised it to him. "*Kanpai!*" she cheered as she tapped her can against his.

London opened his mouth to respond, possibly to ask for a translation, but was interrupted by the whole group cheering back "*Kanpai!*" as they raised their various cans and bottles in the air.

London was pulled away to help light the fireworks that the group had bought along with the alcohol, and John played an upbeat Australian pop song Abigail had not heard before.

She looked out among her co-workers, her friends, and her possible new romantic interest. Despite being surrounded by such wonderful people, an extreme sense of loneliness passed over her. She had dealt with her friends and surrogate family leaving before, but there was something more painful and permanent about this.

If John, who could come up with a way to manage any situation, had only one option left to him, and that was moving away, then how would the rest of the less-than-adventurous of them fare? And if Cheryl felt forced to leave, how soon until Abigail would be following her, maxing out a credit card simply to get back to the country of her birth?

The sky lit up with explosions of light and the park lit up with explosions of laughter and cheering.

Not long after the fireworks display began, the police arrived. While neither fireworks nor being drunk in public were crimes in Japan, drunk *gaijin* setting off fireworks in a public park did raise concerns in the Japanese community.

The officers, who could not understand English, scanned the group for someone who could speak Japanese. Cheryl's "oriental mask" brought their attention to her, and they told her to ask the group to disperse.

Despite Cheryl's Asian appearance, after five years of living in Japan, she communicated mostly in exaggerated hand gestures and a few *arigatou*s and *sumimasen*s. "I'm sorry, I don't understand," she explained.

The two officers looked around hopelessly at the group of foreign faces, then back at Cheryl. "*Nihonjin mitai desu ne? Nihongo wakarimasen ka?*

"I . . . don't . . . understand." She made an "X" with her arms to clarify that she didn't get it.

Abigail decided to diffuse the situation. While her Japanese was not perfect, she could communicate better in Japanese than most locals could communicate in English. Upon seeing her approaching, the officers switched to broken English.

"BOOM, no. Here, no BOOM," they commanded, then turned on their heels and walked away.

Abigail heard them in the distance mumbling in Japanese to one another that the *gaijin* should learn to speak Japanese. Abigail gritted her teeth and turned to the rest of the group.

"Well, you heard the man," she announced. "Here, no BOOM!"

Cheryl laughed and put her arm around Abigail.

"Thank you for that great translation service. Hey, do you guys wanna karaoke, since we're obviously not welcome here anymore? It's past ten, so it's only like 300 yen per person. And of course, that includes all-you-can-drink alcohol."

John looked in his guitar case at his income for the evening. "I have 150 yen, three bottle caps, a cup of ramen and a half-empty can of beer. I'm not complaining, but it looks like I'm not set for karaoke tonight." He laughed as he picked up the beer and took a sip.

London gave John a hearty pat on the back. "I think I can shell out 300 yen for you, man. That's, like, three bucks, right?"

London then looked over at Abigail.

"You'll be going, surely? I can pay for your admission, too, if you want. Since we can't BOOM here."

She was sticky from the hot night and her first instinct was to go home, but if she did the image of London's intent eyes and broad chest would keep her from sleep and make her that much . . . hotter.

"I . . . I . . . guess I can go for a couple hours," she stammered. "But I can shell out my own 300 yen."

"Come on now," London countered and then announced to the group, "karaoke is on me, everyone!"

Cheryl broke in between Abigail and London. "Yay! We're singing 'Hotstepper'!" she cheered, grabbing Abigail's reluctant arm and guiding her in the direction of the glowing neon lights outside the park as the rest of the group followed along.

❧

The neon lights and techno music of the karaoke parlor were a stark contrast to the tranquility and acoustic music of the park, and the group fed off the energy and the free drinks included in the admission price.

They stumbled from the bar down the hallways of rooms all emitting horrible renditions of Japanese pop bands, Britney Spears and the Beatles, until they reached their designated room.

The room was too small for the group, but they moved the table to the side so some of them could sit on the floor. The room spun with noise and heat and alcohol as they all tried to find a place to sit.

When Abigail was finally seated, she felt the newly-familiar weight of an arm around her shoulder and looked up to see London, who was looking through the book of songs to choose from. Her gaze followed his chiseled jaw to his lips. She had only a moment to fantasize about his warm lips on her neck before the lips curled into a crooked smile. He faced her, lowering his eyes to meet hers, and the rest of the room faded away. There was a fire in his eyes that Abigail was sure hers matched, and every muscle in her body tensed.

But there was Cheryl again, excited as ever.

"Abby! It's our turn!"

She yanked Abigail up from her perfect perch and led her to one of the couches, which they climbed on. Standing atop the plush couch, Ini Kamoze's "Here Comes The Hotstepper" music surrounded her.

Cheryl sang with gusto and elbowed Abigail to join in. She reluctantly joined in on the chorus, trying to hide her disappointment over being interrupted . . . for 1990s party music, of all things.

London didn't disappoint, though, proving he could get in on the fun as much as the rest of them. Within seconds, he was standing on the couch next to Abigail singing along, "Still love ya like that . . ."

When the song was nearly finished, a tall, young Japanese man with long spiked hair and wearing the karaoke parlor's uniform walked into the room timidly, carrying a tray.

"Ooh! It's here!" Abigail jumped up to pay the employee before London could get out his wallet.

She set the tray down on the table and the group all started grabbing round pastries from it. London eyed the plate suspiciously.

"What's all this?" he asked.

Abigail popped one into her mouth and picked up another with her fingertips, bringing it close to London's full lips. He parted them without taking his eyes off hers.

"This isn't half bad," he said, looking back at the plate. It was already close to empty. "I think I'll order another plate of them for the group. What are they called?"

"*Takoyaki*. They're octopus balls."

London's mouth dropped open. "Blech . . ."

"Not actually *balls*." She laughed. "Pastry balls with octopus in them."

He simply stared at her . . . not ordering another round.

"Still blech?" she asked.

"*Takoyaki*, then," he said as he got up from the couch.

Before he went through the door leading to the main bar, he turned to Abigail with a crooked smile.

"Tasted good, and heck, you only live once."

❧

The group of teachers began to disperse as soon as they stepped foot outside the karaoke hall, saying their goodnights. Those that lived close to the bigger train stations that ran trains at all hours stumbled toward the train station. Others went in the various directions of their nearby apartments. One guy tried to push off on his bike and immediately fell over, laughed it off, and walked his bike in the direction of home. John and Cheryl spoke quietly, their heads together. She giggled, swatted at his wide shoulder, and then fell into his arms, tilting her head up for a kiss. On John's face Abigail saw through his drunkenness a hint of his surprise at his luck. He had no idea Cheryl held her booze much better than she was letting on. Feigning drunkenness was just as much an excuse as true drunkenness to do things you wouldn't have otherwise admitted to wanting.

The pair turned and began to walk in the same direction, John's arm wrapped around Cheryl's waist.

The street lights swam around Abigail's line of sight, and the sweet clear sake clung to her breath. Still summer air warmed her skin as she looked at her shoes, wondering if she could make shoes out of fabric and humming softly to herself the last tune she'd sung.

London's voice brought her back to herself.

"Never really cools down here, does it?"

"Not in the summer. Just hot and hotter."

"Hot and hotter," London muttered.

Abigail tried to remember if he'd had much to drink. He had bought the drinks and the fireworks that they'd brought to the park. And then the all-you-can-drink sake had flowed from the moment the group entered their karaoke room. She didn't ever overly imbibe, but she had sipped slowly throughout the night.

Had he?

How could she not know the answer? They'd spent the night side by side, sung together, conspired together over the next snack they'd order. Laughed together and generally gravitated toward one another all night. Yet she couldn't picture what he'd been drinking.

"Hot and hotter," she repeated, realizing as the words left her mouth that she was eyeing him like a tigress. Hot and hotter.

And as suddenly as the group had formed in the park, it dissipated. There stood only two *gaijin*, alone but together, in the still night a long ways from home.

London's long fingers traced her jaw, his eyes focused on her slightly-parted lips. He tilted her head up, and his mouth came down, down, down.

Their lips connected as they'd always meant to connect, had finally found their way home. Abigail's head swam, only now the *sake* wasn't to blame.

When London pulled away, her eyes met his smiling ones. She opened her mouth to speak, but she couldn't think of the words to say without sounding too cliché or too desirous.

London slipped his hand around her waist until the palm rested on the small of her back. "Where to now?"

Abigail's pulse raced. She wanted him. She wanted him.

But then, what was it that had caught her thoughts earlier in the day? What was it had that turned her away from his eyes before? When was it?

In the park. When Abigail realized John was leaving and Cheryl was leaving. And that London would leave. Not leave *her*, per se, but leave. Everyone's cash ran out eventually, and he'd have to go back to Maui and leave her here. It wouldn't be his fault. But he'd have to go.

Once more, a sudden wave of loneliness passed over Abigail. The locals saw her as an exotic fetish to use for an hour at a Love Hotel and be through with, and the *gaijin*—her staff and colleagues—would never stay here with her. She'd dodged romance this long without knowing quite why, without realizing the full extent of the hopelessness of her situation.

Finally she answered, "No," and stepped out of London's embrace.

"Did I overstep—"

"No, that's not it. It's . . ."

But what could she say? *You'll leave me* sounded far too needy and would mean something else to him.

". . . it's late and we have work tomorrow."

He stepped toward her, closing in on her.

"Abigail." His voice sounded like waves on rocks.

"Tomorrow," she replied without thinking. Tomorrow what? "Six o'clock. Meet me at . . . Osu Kannon." The words tumbled from her lips.

"Osu Kannon?"

"I'm going to take you to the best *takoyaki* place. It's in Osu Kannon; meet me at the temple there at six."

Abigail straightened her blouse and sucked in a breath of hot night air. Yes. That was it.

London shook his head, smiling his crooked smile. "You are something else, Abigail Dennis. Quite a surprising woman."

"Thanks . . . I guess."

He stared, uncertain, then shrugged. "Heck, everyone trusts you. I suppose I can trust you not to stand me up . . . and not to be exaggerating the octopus balls place."

He laughed again, and she joined in.

"You've never had octopus balls like this."

"Then let me walk you home again and—"

"I can get home . . . it isn't more than a few blocks away."

London grasped her hand, which felt dainty in his large hand. "That's a few blocks more to be with you. I promise I won't invite myself in."

She knew he would leave Nagoya eventually. She knew she shouldn't get attached. But then, what was a little hand-holding? What were a few blocks? So she smiled, squeezed his hand the slightest bit, and allowed him to lead her in the direction of home.

CHAPTER 5

At five minutes to six on Friday, Abigail found London Crane standing in front of a large stone statue at Osu Kannon temple. She approached him from behind and touched his elbow tentatively.

"Abigail," he said, turning, then smiling and leaning down to kiss her cheek. "Is it six already?"

"A few minutes until six. How long have you been waiting?"

"Not long. I know you've been to this temple before, but have you seen this statue?"

She followed his gaze to the towering stone carving on the pedestal. A round-cheeked, cherub-faced couple was carved from the gray stone. They were carved away from the stone, but not away from one another, touching at the cheek, the shoulder, the arm, the hips, and the legs. They were adorable, cartoon-like; they could be children conspiring together had their foreheads been touching instead of their cheeks. His hair receded and hers curled on one side like a sea shell. They weren't children; they were lovers, inseparable. Their lips smiled, and they could have been looking at each other or at the heavens together.

"I've seen it before," she replied, but then added, "but I don't know if I've ever really *looked* at it. It's very sweet, isn't it?"

"Yeah," he said without looking away from the statue. "How could you not like a statue like that? Do you think they're looking at each other?"

"I'm not sure."

"At first I thought so. But look again. I don't think they are. They're so close they're like one person looking out at the world."

Abigail looked again, thinking that was the way love should be. Not two people struggling to maintain their love, but two people facing the world together. Her eyes trailed from the statue to London, to his wide shoulders under his crisp teal button-up shirt, the sleeves rolled to his elbows. He must not have had time to change after work, she thought as she examined his black slacks. Maybe she should have set the time for later. But then again . . . he sure did look *good*.

"That's how love ought to be, so you've got to be right." She flashed him a smile when he turned to look at her. "So, are you ready for some excellent *takoyaki*?"

"I don't know how your schedule looks tonight, but is there time to look around the temple?"

"Of course . . ." Her reply was breathless. One of her favorite parts of living in Japan was the seemingly endless places to temple-hop, but her peers tended to prefer the more urban areas, such as the Osu arcade, the place she'd planned to walk through with London to reach the eatery. But he wanted to see the temple.

"It really is amazing, isn't it? Do you know much about it?" London asked as they moved to the steep, twenty-seven-step staircase that led to the main temple.

Long, narrow banners hung at the railings every few steps, white with red icons and black *kanji*.

"Um, yeah. I guess I do. For example, that red symbol on all these banners . . . see the one that looks like a flower with five circle-petals around it? That's the plum blossom crest of *Tenjin-sama*, um, Sugawara Michizane, a god of learning, or of education. The shrine's dedicated to him."

At the top of the steps loomed the impressive white and orange-red structure, with a sweeping roof line and deep gray tile shingles. Yellow accents at the tips of some orange-red painted wood beams suggested even further depth.

As they climbed the steps, Abigail continued, "This was originally built in the 1300s, but it was in a different village. It was moved to Osu in the 1600s."

"Why did they move it here?" he asked when they reached the top. He moved toward a black iron grating and pit from which incense rose.

Abigail thought the curl of smoke that rose across London's chest before dissipating looked like a visual of his soul curling around his core. His heart.

"Security, I think," she replied, realizing her own security measures were toppling with every moment she lingered in conversation with London in such close physical proximity.

He leaned over the incense pit and commented, "Interesting. It doesn't smell like the incense they sell in stores back home. I mean, the perfumed kind the girls get to set the mood in their apartments."

He chuckled and shook his head.

"It isn't for romance, of course. The incense is supposed to represent the breath of the gods."

She wondered how many girls had tried to "set the mood" for London. His laugh suggested that he hadn't been impressed, and Abigail knew that so often women set a mood that was romantic to themselves only. Not that all a guy needed was a woman to take off her clothes to get him in the mood. But then again, seduction with skin was usually more effective than seduction with candles and rose petals.

Abigail looked up at the gold-lettered signage on the umber-colored background.

"The pagoda burned down in a big fire in the 1800s," she said absently, "but it was rebuilt in the 1970s."

London's reply was just as absent. "Usually when things are destroyed they're rebuilt. It's one of the hard things to remember right after destruction. What are these candles for?"

She moved to his side next to the glass case filled with thin black pegs, some supporting narrow white candles.

"People light them and say a prayer," she explained, motioning to the words on the case. "They're 200 yen each. Some places let them burn out, but some temples have someone who goes around and blows them out. That always sits weirdly with me, but then again, I'm not Buddhist, so what do I know?"

London took another look around. "You know a lot about temples for someone who isn't Buddhist."

She shrugged. "I like them, like the architecture, the art of them. And the spaces so often feel spiritual, calming. This one is a little more urban. But you should see the ones set in natural places. I like those best, for relaxing and regrouping, I mean."

"I'd like to see those temples."

"Then maybe I'll be your tour guide someday."

"Why can't someday be tomorrow?" he asked as they moved back to the staircase and toward the large white and orange-red trimmed gate.

Someday. Stay a while, she thought. But she replied, "We'll see. For now, are you ready for some *takoyaki* or what?"

"Bring on the octopus balls."

London held out his arm gallantly and she took it, with a quick glance up at his crooked grin.

❧

"It's like a labyrinth in here," London observed just minutes after entering the arcade area of Osu.

And it was, with its twisting, turning alleyways. One tiny shop-front after another lined the narrow pedestrian street, and crowded displays in front of each made it difficult to distinguish one shop from another.

"Yeah, but look at these great shops."

Abigail was walking slightly in front of London, leading him by the hand, guiding him in the foot traffic around them. She turned back to face him briefly.

"If you want to pick up cheap souvenirs to take home with you, this is a great place."

"I'll remember that someday in the future when I go home." He squeezed her hand. "For now, I'm happy to just be here with you."

She smiled, and London's face showed that he recognized the hint of sadness she couldn't cover up. She motioned at white paper signs in front of a clothing shop. The advertisement was in *kanji* but large red numbers stood out.

¥ 300
¥ 500
¥ 800

"These are great prices on shirts if you want to take a look."

"A three-dollar shirt?" London raised an eyebrow skeptically. "I'm not pretentious about my clothing, Abigail, but come on."

She swatted his arm, the mood lightening, knowing as soon as he saw these shirts his feelings about them would change. Abigail rustled through the rack and pulled out a white hoodie, the zipper pulled up, the back toward London.

"This might look good on you," she said with a mischievous grin.

"I told you, I can afford—"

But Abigail turned the shirt with a movement full of gusto, revealing the front. In thick gold English script it read: *Leave it to that person.*

London stared, brow furrowed.

"What . . . what does that even mean?"

"What do you mean? It means *leave it to that person*!"

London broke into laughter. "That doesn't mean anything! Who checked that for grammar?"

"No one did, that's the great thing about shirts in Japan with English writing! Think about how many people back home wear shirts or have tattoos of *kanji* based on what someone told them it means! These are just bad translations. The point isn't the words, but how the font looks on a shirt."

London pulled out a woman's shirt, olive green with white Old English font. "Oh, wow . . . Abigail . . . check this one out."

She reached for it, but he held on, reading aloud.

Time takes a cigarette, puts it in your mouth, the wall-to-wall is calling, then you forget you're a rock and roll suicide.

"Poetic."

London was already looking through the rack again, and Abigail realized she was quite glad he could see the humor. How could she expect to have a good time with someone who didn't find these shirts fantastic?

She couldn't see what he was looking at, but she saw him smirk.

"What did you find?"

"Ummm . . ."

She reached over, trying to see what he was looking at, but he pulled the black t-shirt off the rack and held it with the front against his chest.

"Well, come on. Now you have to let me see."

"I think I'm going to get this one. I think it'll fit. I don't know what it means really, but it sounds awesome."

Still he wouldn't show her, and he went to the cashier to pay for the shirt.

"The suspense is killing me," she sighed with a roll of the eyes, heading back to the alley.

The transaction sure was taking a long time, she thought. Usually it was a quick hand-over-the-yen-and-you're-done kind of thing. Abigail wondered if he was trying to haggle on the price. He hadn't been paid, after all, since moving here. She decided she'd pay for the *takoyaki*, for sure.

When London re-emerged, the teal work shirt was thrown over his forearm and he was wearing a thin cotton, fitted black shirt. Abigail's breath caught at the way it clung to his wide shoulders and chest, his tight stomach, his narrow waist. He'd tucked it into his black slacks. Add a pair of shades and he'd look fresh from Hollywood.

"I asked the guy if I could change my shirt in there. I don't think he knew what he was agreeing to, because he looked shocked when I started to take off my shirt." London laughed heartily. "So what do you think?"

He held out his arms, allowing her to take him in.

Abigail reluctantly drew her eyes from his stomach, up toward his chest, to read the words.

Slow Hand Jam

She felt the heat rise to her face. "My goodness."

London's crooked smile dropped. "Not funny?"

"No . . . no . . . it is . . ."

He held the shirt out, examining the text upside-down. "I don't get it. It doesn't make sense, but I thought it was cool."

"It is . . ."

"Does it . . . mean something I'm not getting?"

Abigail swallowed, calmed herself, and managed a laugh. "No, I don't think so. It means as much as the other shirts, I guess. It's just that . . . well, doesn't it seem kind of sexy?"

She could hardly believe she'd said it aloud.

"Does it?" London's voice carried a tone of joking disbelief.

She rolled her eyes and laughed off the tension. "Oh, geez. You sure do go for the effect, don't you?"

"Come on, though, it's a great shirt."

She scanned the shirt again. Scanned the body the shirt clung to.

"It sure is."

"These are some good octopus balls, despite the name," London said with a crooked smile before taking another bite.

"Told you," she replied, still the slightest bit shaky from his tight shirt, and what it hinted lay underneath it.

"So, you've been here five years. And I've only seen you eating Japanese food. Granted, I haven't watched you eat very often."

"You're not peeking in my kitchen window each morning and night? But it is true, I mainly eat Japanese food. It's just easier that way, and cheaper."

"And is there anything you really miss from home? For example, I can't imagine going five years without a really good slice of fresh pineapple. Or a burrito."

"As though you have good burritos in Maui!" She laughed. "Come to San Diego, and I'll show you real Mexican food."

"Fine, let's go right now."

"In your private jet?"

"If you want to, but I'm not usually that extravagant, Abigail."

"Back to your question. First of all, I *have* been home for visits in the past five years. I go back the last week of each year. The school closes for the New Year holiday and so it's the perfect time."

"Nice. Maybe I can plan a vacation for New Year's, too. That way I don't have to take unpaid time off."

Despite herself, Abigail joined him in laughing. She was sure there was no way he'd last the winter, let alone past summer, but that didn't mean the joke wasn't a good one.

"Even though we've got all these great hole-in-the-wall Mexican restaurants at home, the first thing I want to eat every time I get home is pizza."

"Really? I'm sure I've seen pizza places here."

"Yeah, but have you eaten at them? They put mayo on everything. It just isn't the same. I'm not really picky about pizza, but these are pretty bad."

"Tell me more about home."

"What is there to tell? My parents are still in San Diego. I have two younger sisters."

"Ah, I've got sisters too. Three. They are all in the hotel business, like I am. Or was. What do your sisters do?"

Abigail couldn't help thinking he would be back in hospitality when he had to go home. Would the people whose jobs he'd tried to save still be there? Would he just find a new job?

"Both are still in school. One's a freshman at Cal State Fullerton, and the other is a senior at Vanguard University of Southern California. Both schools are in Orange County, so they carpool home to San Diego to do laundry and eat home cooking. I'm the only one who's more than an hour away. I miss them a lot, but I do feel good about what I'm doing."

"You should. Not only teaching your students, but looking out for your staff, too. Since you have two younger siblings, I'm guessing you've always been kind of—"

"Bossy?"

"Maybe so! I was going to say '*a caregiver.*'"

Abigail stared at her chopsticks and sighed. "A whole lot of good it's done the people I'm trying to watch out for. All these great teachers without pay, some forced to head home. And it isn't like the economy is great in the States or England or Australia or anywhere they're from. They're going back to a place where they probably won't be able to find jobs. And those are the lucky ones. Some don't even have the money to go home, like John. He wasn't busking the other night just for the hell of it, or to buy some new gadget or take a weekend trip to Tokyo— that's what he used to do maybe a year ago. Nope, he's just trying to raise enough cash to survive."

The conversation had taken a turn Abigail hadn't expected. London looked at his chopsticks, and she wondered if he worried about running out of cash too. Would his parents bail him out? And how awkward would that be? He must be in his late twenties. Perhaps he was trying to calculate how much longer he could stay before getting out of Dodge with enough money for a plane ticket home.

"Sorry," she apologized. "I didn't mean to vent that way."

"You weren't even venting for yourself," he said, half smiling. "You're more worried about your staff. What are *your* plans?"

She sighed, set down her chopsticks, and leaned back in her chair, stretching luxuriously.

"Who knows?" she replied with more honesty than she had given to others who'd posed the same question to her.

"Will you go back to San Diego?"

"I'd rather not. I mean, I really do love it here. I'll probably try to find another job."

"Are the teaching jobs filling up because of English World's issues?"

"Yeah, at least in the cities where English World had outposts. All the big cities. But I may be able to get another headmistress position. Or move to a smaller town or village. I haven't really looked for a job, to be honest. I didn't think I needed to, until . . ."

Her voice trailed off and she focused on him. It wasn't until London had shown up that it even crossed her mind that she'd have to be seriously thinking about this.

"Until?"

"Until you gave me a much-needed dose of reality."

London smiled faintly. "Wouldn't my folks be happy to hear that? London Crane, living in the real world. I didn't even realize I'd leaned that way."

"What do you mean, didn't realize it? You're the one who pointed out that English World was not to be trusted, or trusted so blindly."

"My folks think I have my head in the clouds, is all. Too casual. Too relaxed. No business sense. They'd be happy to hear I wasn't just going with the flow for once."

"So what's your story, then? Tell me about *your* family."

London pushed his plate away and patted his stomach, as though he were full. Abigail couldn't help noticing the washboard abs under his black *Slow Hand Jam* t-shirt looked no less taut than it did before the *takoyaki*.

"Can we save that for another day? I'm ready to move around, work this off. And there are so many issues with my family that, ah, that belong to some other time."

"Fair enough," she replied, and reached into her purse.

He stayed her hand. "I got it."

"No, come on. I can get it."

He shook his head.

"At least," she protested, "let me pay half."

"Nope. Put your wallet away. Please let me get this."

Abigail placed her wallet back in her purse. She was thankful for his politeness, but slightly annoyed. She couldn't put her finger on the reason at that moment, but as they exited the building and he held the door for her, she realized her fear was that every yen he spent was another moment closer to him leaving. And besides, hadn't she fended for herself rather well over the last five years?

They walked along the alleyways, poking their heads into a shop front here and there to view Nintendo-themed action figures, *manga* and figures based on the characters, and second-hand electronics. When they'd made it to the edge of the arcade and walked back into the courtyard of Osu Kannon, London turned to face her.

She wasn't sure how she'd answer if he were to ask her again, *Where to now?* as he had last night. So instead, she asked, "Was the *takoyaki* worth the trip?"

"Spending the evening with you was worth it."

"And I'm sure the purchase of that great shirt was an added bonus."

He pulled the shirt slightly away from his body and looked down at the words.

"Sure was!"

When he looked up and flashed Abigail a crooked grin, releasing the shirt so that it snapped back against his chest, she felt the temple around her teeter. And tonight, she hadn't had any *sake*.

London spoke again. "I especially liked this temple, actually. It was so interesting to explore, and it has such beautiful architecture. Do you know of other temples this nice?"

Did she ever! Abigail had spent nearly every weekend of her first year here temple-hopping, exploring every temple she could find in a book and every shrine mentioned by the other teachers. She'd even taken some weekend trips to explore temples in other cities and villages.

"I do."

"I was trying to bait you into offering to show me some."

"I told you already I would."

"I don't mean someday. I mean now."

"Such urgency," she cooed. "It's a little late to do it tonight. But how about next weekend? I know just the ones I want to show you."

London stepped in closer, grasping both of her hands in his. "Then, hmmm, what shall we do tonight?"

She tilted her head, accepting his lips as they met hers hungrily. One arm wrapped around her waist, the hand pressing the small of her back, urging her toward him.

She placed one palm on his chest, covering *Slow* on his shirt. Under his t-shirt his chest was pure muscle, firm, unyielding. Abigail lowered her head and pressed her cheek on his chest; she could hear the rapid thud-thud of his heartbeat. He was as excited as she.

But as her hand dropped to his narrow waist, the word on the t-shirt was re-exposed.

Slow.

She stepped aside.

"I should go home."

"Is it the shirt?" he asked with a crooked grin, as though he thought she were joking, or at least playing coy, but would ultimately join him at his place.

"It isn't that . . ."

"So, you *do* want to come home for a Slow Hand Jam?"

She laughed in spite of herself, in spite of the last shred of her willpower that was so desperately trying to hold firm.

"London . . . ," she started, and his smile dropped.

"That doesn't sound good."

"Please let me finish."

His arm dropped from her back, though one hand tentatively held her hand.

"London, I'm not the kind of person who just . . . *falls* into bed with anyone."

"Anyone? Neither am I, Abigail. And I don't think of you as *just anyone*. I really enjoy being with you, in case you hadn't noticed."

"Same here. But this is a little quick for me."

"It *feels* right on time," he protested.

Too much more of his sandpapery voice and she'd crumble beneath its persuasion. She needed to get away. Or she needed to tell the whole truth.

"Maybe that 'right on time' that you're feeling—that urgency—is because you won't be here much longer."

"You keep bringing that up. And I keep telling you I'm okay. I have enough to stay a while. I'm not going to work for free forever, but if you and I . . . ," he squeezed her hand, ". . . if there is anything here, I won't go home."

"That is very sweet, very sweet. But I've seen the most dedicated folks go home. You can't live here without money. And teaching jobs are going to those people who've been teaching for years with English World, not to a brand new teacher, fresh off the boat."

"Will you stop worrying about me?"

"I'm worrying about . . ." What was she worrying about? Herself?

"About what? About me leaving you? After we've only known each other a week or so?"

"Too soon to worry about you leaving, but not too soon to sleep together?" Her voice caught at the end. She'd said it aloud. And in this context, it no longer sounded all that inviting.

London crossed his arms over his chest. "So what? You want to see my bank balances? Want to do my numbers and see how long I'll be with you and if it will be long enough to warrant making love? How much do I need to have in my account for you to want to sleep with me?"

She was surprised at the fire in his voice. She hadn't heard him so defensive since their first conversation on the train.

"Of course not," she countered, holding her chin up.

"If that's what matters to you, I'll pull up my statements tonight. And while it may ease your concerns, Abigail, it will also mean you're not the kind of woman I thought you were."

"Don't you *dare* tell me what kind of woman I am," she replied, as fired up now as he. "I took care of myself and my staff for years before you showed up. And don't you *dare* try to show me your *bank statements,* for goodness sakes! I won't say I've never been more insulted, because I get a lot of crazy comments here, but to insinuate that I'd sleep with you based on your bank account is right up there."

"If it doesn't matter, then why are so you concerned about when my money's going to run out?"

"Because I don't want to get attached!"

London's shoulders relaxed. He touched her arm lightly. "So if it really isn't about money, then how can I prove to you that I'm not planning to use you and leave? I've given you no evidence that that's in my character, but obviously you're assuming I'm going to."

"Not that you'll plan to."

"But that I'm going to."

The tension in Abigail's body eased now, too, and she realized she was tired. "Next weekend we'll go temple-hopping. I know just the places to take you. For now, please, I have to get home."

"Yeah, that's fine. I think the moment's passed." He smiled.

"I did have a good time tonight." She pulled away and took a few steps back. "And . . . great shirt!"

He leaned in and kissed her on the forehead. Then she turned and walked briskly toward the train station, hoping he wouldn't follow. The entire way she cursed herself for being so harsh with him. Couldn't she have been just a little more eloquent in her explanation? Sound a little less needy and frigid?

Because she was anything but needy. She'd gotten along this long without a man in her life. She didn't *need* him, for sex or for anything. Just because she didn't want to give it up for a guy she didn't know very well didn't make her needy.

And she was anything but *frigid*.

Through her weariness, she realized her skin was still aflame from their kiss. She'd been so close to going home with him. She could have been in his arms at this moment, on the way to his bed.

She fanned her face with her hand. She'd done the right thing.

If so, why were her surroundings spinning as she walked? Why was she warmer than the air around her?

Why was every inch of her body tingling with regret?

Between the train station and her apartment, Abigail's cell phone rang. She wondered if it might be London calling, giving one more push to their being together tonight. And she caught herself hoping it was him. Caught herself thinking she might say yes.

But the photo that popped up on the phone showed a red-cheeked, strawberry blonde with her long hair in a high ponytail, a smile showing two rows of perfectly straight teeth. She'd mentioned the hated braces of her high school years the first time they'd met, when Abigail complimented her smile.

At the time, Abigail had been the administrative head for Nagoya schools for a year, and the woman who was destined to become a close friend and valuable colleague had just been promoted and was Abigail's Osaka counterpart. After the annual corporate board meeting in Tokyo at which they first met, they'd spent the next two days at Tokyo DisneySea, sharing a hostel nearby and enjoying the adventure at the park.

Though this call certainly wasn't London, it was just as welcome.

Abigail flipped open the phone. "Savannah Thompson! You've finally decided to respond, have you?"

"Finally is right! You emailed me a couple days ago, but . . . have you been up to your ears in work, Abby? I mean, the handful of teachers I have left—and I do mean handful—are not the most committed folks, understandably so. I end up scheduling classes to teach every day of the week because I'm the only one I know who will actually show up. I haven't had a weekend in a month!"

"Savannah . . . you can run the school yourself just fine, but you can't run it *and* do the work for all the teachers, too. You're going to burn out."

"What do you mean *going to* burn out?" Savannah sucked in a breath, possibly the first one since Abigail answered. Her hurried sentences gave weight to her rushed words.

"I know I wrote that we should brainstorm ideas on how to handle the situation, but if your idea is for me to teach all the classes myself," Abigail said, "then this conversation is over. I'm dedicated, but not insane. Speaking of, is Osaka insanely hot and humid this summer?"

"As always."

"Nagoya, too. My gosh, I've been here five years and every summer I'm shocked."

"And every winter you're shocked by the cold."

"True."

"Have you been here five years, truly?"

Abigail reached the front door of the apartment complex and pulled it open. Before she closed it, she took a quick glance outside, hardly registering what she saw. She slipped her shoes off and kicked them into the corner with the shoes of the tenants of the three other apartments. She slid the key into the lock and stepped in.

What had she seen outside? The thought crossed her mind as soon as the door clicked shut, and she hastily turned the lock. Was it her imagination, or had someone been standing across the street from the house? And if so, why did it give her a sudden chill? They could be standing there for any number of reasons.

"Five years."

Abigail looked around her apartment. Five years and she'd hardly settled in at all. Until recently, she knew her fear of losing her work visa was a little exaggerated. But now, with English World in trouble . . .

"And my three years feels like forever these days. But that's the circumstances, I think. That's all. So, Abby, you've obviously not been taking all the classes for your schools. How are you covering them?"

"Not well. I still have some teachers around, but the ranks are dwindling. Fewer show up each day. Can't blame them. I cover some classes, and we overbook the others. Lot of standing-room-only classes last week. I just don't have much more wiggle room."

"I know what you mean. I'm going to have to simply close the school here pretty soon."

Abigail toyed with the notebook on the counter holding the start of what would become the lesson plan for the week. "I feel for the students. They've already paid. The high schoolers have exams coming up."

"We've done what we can."

Savannah's words suggested resolution, but Abigail heard her voice crack. A lump rose in Abigail's throat, for her friend even more than the situation.

Why should they be so emotionally affected by something they were not responsible for? Were not in control of?

Then again, perhaps that was just it. They had no control.

"So no tips?"

"Just do what you can, I guess. And if you have to close down the schools, or cut classes, do it and know it isn't your fault."

Abigail sighed and shut the notebook, but didn't respond.

"When did—"

Savannah stopped mid-sentence, as though she'd changed her mind about saying it. But Abigail urged her to speak her mind.

"When did what?"

"Oh," Savannah sighed, "when did we go from being two women at the top of their game, living in an exotic place, doing what we love, making a difference . . . to two women at a loss for the next step in their own lives, let alone the next steps for the people they want to help." She paused, and then tagged on at the end, "That's all."

Abigail didn't know what to say, her friend's hopelessness weighing down her own heart. It was only a moment before Savannah had regained composure.

"Have you thought of taking that offer from English World?"

"What offer?"

"You know. The one they mailed out to the administrative heads?"

Abigail looked at her mail pile. She'd opened and sorted it all.

"I didn't get anything from them. What is it?"

She heard Savannah shuffle some papers, and then there was a pause, as though she were skimming the paperwork.

"They sent me an offer to go away for a while. Didn't say where, but it sounds like a resort or something. Or maybe they'll send me home if I ask them to. They're worried that I could be a target, with Mr. Inudori missing and all. They've offered it to . . . oh, I guess it is just a few people they sent it to. The ones they think could be in danger if someone is upset with English World."

"I guess they don't think I'm a target?"

"Guess not. I wonder if that means they have some lead that the person who kidnapped Inudori is from Osaka."

Abigail sat down on a kitchen chair, leaned on an elbow resting on the table. "Geez, Savannah. That's sort of creepy, isn't it?"

"Not really. I think it is kind of them to offer. They can't have much money to do this. But it does seem rather extreme. I mean, Inudori is pretty far up the food chain. And if he was kidnapped by someone in Osaka, the culprit has got to know how hard I've been working to keep the school afloat."

"Yeah, I mean, even if English World doesn't realize it."

"I won't toss it yet, in case you get an offer. If you do though, and we end up having to close our schools, then let's get out of Dodge together, okay?"

Abigail smiled. "We'll see if it comes to that."

But she knew she wasn't going to leave because of work. Things *outside* of work were just getting interesting.

CHAPTER 6

"Mamonaku . . . ichiban Meijo senno, Motoyama . . . Motoyama desu," said the stationmaster, announcing over the P.A. system the arrival of the next subway train. The burst of air from the coming car lifted Abigail's knee-length floral skirt, bringing blessed relief from the hot, still air of the subway station.

Abigail sat on a bench facing the subway arrival platform that London should arrive on and glanced down at her watch: 1:59 p.m.

She re-checked the text messages on her phone. She'd touched base with London last night with a casual message that did not indicate the excitement she felt as she looked forward to the day with him, all the possibilities.

Have to get some work done in the morning, but if you're still up for temple-hopping, meet me at Motoyama station off the Meijo line at two o'clock, and wear comfortable walking shoes.

He'd responded with a resounding, *Definitely! I'll be there!*

She closed her phone and remembered her biting words.

Too soon to worry about you leaving, but not too soon to sleep together?

She'd been too harsh with him, she decided. But was he really so vindictive as to agree to plans with her, then stand her up?

"Whatever," she muttered, trying to brace herself for a no-show. "I enjoyed temple-hopping on my own long before he got here, and I'll be enjoying it long after he leaves."

She smoothed her tank top and reached into her over-sized bag to pull out the Eliza Tahan book she was so close to finishing. Her sister had picked it up back home and sent it in the last care package of American luxuries, along with deodorant and taco shells. She glanced at her watch: 2:05.

On the outskirts of Nagoya the trains came only once every ten minutes, and she decided to give him two more trains before heading out to enjoy the temple on her own. She opened *Sands of Botswana* and the smell of home, absorbed into the paper, filled her senses.

She couldn't say that she longed for home the way many of her peers did. Sure, she missed her family and the consistent 75-degree San Diego weather, but Nagoya *felt* like home. She missed San Diego in the way an adult misses her childhood home; moving back was not an option, but it was still pleasant to remember and to visit.

A familiar jingle hinted at the arrival of the next train, and the stationmaster confirmed it. Abigail smoothed the hair at her temples and checked that it was still neatly tucked back behind her headband. She attempted to look uninterested in the approaching train.

The usually packed train was nearly empty this Saturday afternoon, and London's towering frame stood out. Abigail smiled and watched him look out the window at the platform, lost until his eyes met hers. A crooked smile spread across his face as he rushed off the train just before the automatic doors closed and he jogged up to embrace Abigail.

She slipped *Sands of Botswana* back into her bag and pushed London back playfully.

"I thought you'd stood me up after I'd planned this whole day out for you."

He bowed deeply in traditional Japanese businessman fashion.

"*Gomen nasai,* Abigail-*sama.*"

This broke Abigail from her angry façade into full laughter. He'd only been in Japan for a couple weeks and already he could be sarcastic in Japanese. *Sama* was a suffix the Japanese added to the name of someone they hold in high respect, like a prime minister or an emperor. It had mostly been dropped in modern conversation . . . except for sarcasm.

"Wow! A couple weeks ago you couldn't pronounce your train station and now you're making fun of me in Japanese? Impressive, indeed!"

"I still took the train the wrong way! But at least my Japanese classes are teaching me enough to get a laugh out of you."

"Japanese classes?" Was he really so vested in staying that he was shelling out dough for Japanese classes? Maybe she'd been too quick to assume he'd leave.

"Sure. I don't have anything else to do at night . . . yet."

He ran his fingers down her bare arm and interlaced them with hers, never breaking eye contact. She imagined his fingers exploring her bare body as her eyes explored his smooth tanned skin from under his pressed, short-sleeve fitted shirt. Her eyes fell to his toned calves under a pair of shorts, realizing this was the first time she'd seen his tanned legs.

"You said you'd be my guide today." His voice dropped to a suggestive whisper. "So guide me."

She wanted to guide him right back to her apartment, onto her futon, under her tank top and flowing skirt. She blushed and shook the image of his bare chest from her head, looking up with a smile.

"And guide you I shall."

❧

"This wasn't the tour I was expecting when you invited me temple-hopping," London said as the couple reached the top of a hilly street lined with fast food joints and department stores.

"Such urgency, London Crane. Just wait and see."

He walked ahead, read an advertisement on a fast food restaurant and started laughing. Abigail hurried to look on.

"Is this the shrine you want to take me to? Mos Burger?"

She followed his gaze to a poster with a holy-looking hand palm up with a small hamburger in it. Under the hand the caption read, "Burger is life."

She laughed, too. "No, but you're getting warmer."

She pointed to a small opening between Mos Burger and a wall and walked toward it.

The opening was barely wide enough for them to walk side by side. The walls on either side were twenty feet high and vine-covered stone. A canopy of green nearly blocked out the sky.

London traced his hand along the wall thoughtfully and looked up. "How can this world exist right next door to a Mos Burger?"

"Welcome to the beautiful contradiction that is Japan."

She could tell that London appreciated it the way she did. He hadn't yet entered the temple grounds and he was already enthralled.

"How did you find this place? Are you a big Mos Burger fan, or is it a famous site?"

She paused before speaking, remembering the bright banners and lanterns lining the corridor the evening she'd discovered what soon became one of her favorite temples in Nagoya.

"It was my first spring here. I was just on a bike ride enjoying the moderate weather. Believe it or not, the weather here can be good for about three weeks a year."

"I'll believe it when I feel it."

"It was evening and I saw two women in traditional summer *kimonos* turn into this corridor ahead of me. I slowed down to ogle their beautiful clothes and saw this entryway lit up with lanterns. It was so mystical, like a passageway that could take you to some enchanted place."

"I'd like to see that."

"Well, stay in Japan until May and I'll take you," Abigail urged, before continuing with her memory. "I parked my bike in front of the Mos Burger and followed them in. I think that's when I really fell for Japan. Though it looked like an enchanted passageway, of course I didn't believe that it really was. But when I walked through this corridor here and I passed through that gate there, I was surrounded by a Japan different than I had experienced the five months prior. All the stressed out, tired, suit-clad businessmen I taught during the day—the ones who rarely saw their families—were all there, dressed in loose-fitting cotton robes, smiling, with their children sitting on their shoulders.

"There were vendors selling the most delicious street food I've ever tasted and while I was the only foreigner there—the only *gaijin*—for once no one gawked at my skin. That was back when my Japanese was limited, but that didn't seem to matter, either. An old Japanese woman adopted me for the evening, showing me around and teaching me the traditions and customs while in a temple. She spoke completely in Japanese and, despite the language barrier, I was able to understand what she was trying to communicate. Not only that, but I felt I was understood as well. Like we transcended language, you know?"

"It sounds amazing. I almost feel like I was there."

"So, that's the story. I stumbled on my first traditional festival here. It holds a special place in my heart. And I still think it's a gorgeous temple, with or without all the festivities."

London smiled and squeezed her hand as they walked toward the white, red-trimmed, pagoda-esque gate at the entrance of the temple. The red and white contrasted with the lush greenery on the temple grounds. There were no people in sight, but the temple was alive with cicada song and birds drinking out of tea offerings to statues.

They entered the courtyard of the temple. The temple building was all tones of natural wood. Five pairs of shoes were neatly lined up outside the slightly open temple door. A dim light and the smell of incense flowed through the open door.

"What do you think is going on?" London asked, guiding Abigail closer to the door.

They peeked in from around the door to see a room lined with *tatami* straw flooring and wood and gold figurines ordaining a place of worship. One man and two women were sitting off to the side on their knees with their heads bowed. In the front of the room, a young man lit incense on an altar while he stood next to a young woman. She was holding a small child, whom she passed to him, trading the child for the flame he held and taking a turn lighting the incense. Then they both bowed their heads, the child looking around the dim room with wide eyes before becoming transfixed on London and Abigail peering in. The child was the only one in the room that seemed to notice them.

"It's like a baptism, I think," Abigail whispered to London without taking her eyes off the scene. "I've never seen one, but students have explained it to me before. There's a Buddhist ceremony for birth and death, but most other ceremonies are executed by the Shinto religion, which believes every little thing is sacred."

The young couple sat back down near the spectators. One of the spectators then stood up and approached the altar, lighting another incense stick and bowing her head.

"Family members offer up their prayers for the child and the family individually. I don't think it's about offering the child's soul as in a Christian baptism, but rather praying the child will have the tools to live a full life."

Abigail nuzzled up closer to London and his clean, musky scent blended well with the incense. She could feel herself opening up to him more than she had planned. She knew that if he left even now, she'd let him in too far not to feel his absence. It was too late now, and so there was no point in holding back. As it had been for the Japanese businessmen who celebrated here during that spring festival so many years ago, the essence of the place had erased her defenses.

She peered up at London, who had been staring at her with his aqua eyes. He kissed her forehead and held her closer.

After each family member had taken a turn, a bald monk with a black robe and purple sash closed the doors of the temple completely. London and Abigail turned their backs to the temple building, monastic chanting drifting around them.

Opposite the temple building, a staircase descended into more green. They followed the three-flight descent mindlessly.

"So, I know we talked about this a little before, but have you thought any more about what you'll do if English World really goes down? Will you leave me and go home?" London raised an eyebrow, hoping Abigail would find it humorous.

Abigail furrowed her eyebrows. "What? Do you want to see my bank statements?"

They laughed together.

"I don't have to *go* home," she continued, looking around the temple grounds. "I *am* home."

"I guess after five years a place becomes home, eh?"

She tripped over a fallen branch and grabbed onto London to keep from falling.

"I gotcha."

"Thanks. You know, I actually did some half-hearted research late last night, but couldn't find what I was looking for."

He raised an eyebrow.

"You know it's time to jump ship when Abigail Dennis of all people starts looking for another job. What are you looking for?"

"I'm not jumping ship." She swatted his shoulder, trying to decide if she should mention the conversation with Savannah. She decided against it. She wasn't seriously considering something new, and she didn't want to get him thinking of leaving. She'd stick to answering the question he'd asked.

"I'd actually love to do some nonprofit work. There are a lot of Japanese kids who can't get into a decent high school because they can't afford English World or Math World or whatever world. But Japan isn't exactly big on nonprofits."

"Have you thought about—whoa!" London stopped at the bottom of the stairs and craned his neck up. "That is one big Buddha!"

Abigail craned her neck along with him. The green, iron Buddha figure was flanked by two thirty-story buildings, both of which he towered over. He was seated in a teaching lotus position, with robed monks and five-foot elephants at his feet.

"It's *pretty* big, but I've seen bigger," Abigail bragged.

London laughed and gathered her up in his arms, "Oh, so you just show me moderately big Buddhas? Next time, I expect you to give me a tour of the temple with the biggest Buddha in Japan!

"What are those sculptures over there?" London asked, indicating a hill with hundreds of pointed stone markers as they were exiting the temple.

"Oh, those are grave markers. Do you want to go look at them?"

"Do you mind?"

Abigail grabbed his hand excitedly and hurried toward the cemetery. She had always loved looking through Japanese cemeteries. She had learned many of the *kanji* characters she knew from reading inscriptions, but she had not wanted to scare London off with her love of grave markers.

They walked hand in hand through the maze of stone markers, flowers and food and drink offerings to ancestors. Abigail read off the inscriptions of the more interesting markers.

"This one has been here since the sixteenth century. Each one of these markings is another family member that died. The most recent one was last year."

"Did someone leave a beer on this family's grave?"

London leaned down to pick up the beer can. She stayed his hand.

"It's an offering. The person who died must've liked beer."

"That's my kind of offering!"

They followed the thin path along the hill. London stopped in front of a black stone marker with less writing than the others. Some of the writing was red.

"This one's cool. Almost looks like modern art."

Abigail joined him, tracing the red lettering with a fingertip.

"When a spouse dies, both the husband and wife's names are engraved on the stone. During the funeral ceremony, the surviving spouse traces the name in red paint, as a reminder to meet there when they pass on."

She removed her hand from the marker, but not her gaze. London wrapped his arm around her and eyed the fresh flowers and fruit on the ledge.

"Every time I see the red lettering I imagine how difficult it must be for the surviving spouse to be without their other half."

London disagreed. "I like it. It's so optimistic. 'See you later,' instead of the 'goodbye' Western traditions seem to force loved ones to say at funerals."

Abigail smiled up at him. "When you think of it that way, it's kind of romantic."

He bent down, his hand cupping her face as their lips met. The warmth of the connection made the warm evening air chill.

Abigail's heart opened as her lips parted to let London in.

⁂

Abigail woke to a gentle jerk and then a soaring sensation. She opened her eyes to find London carrying her out of the train car.

"Nice of you to join the land of the living," London teased. "This is your station, right? Rock Band Cho."

"Rokuban-cho. Roo-coo-bon-cho," Abigail corrected him as she slid out of his arms and stood up. "I never sleep through my stop. I'm glad you were there with me."

She stretched her arms above her head and smacked her lips. London wrapped an arm around her waist and she leaned in close as they made their way up the stairs of Rokuban-cho Station.

"Oh! But you missed your stop!" she announced as she realized it.

"I don't miss it that much."

His crooked smile flashed across his face as his large hand dropped to the small of her back, guiding her out the door of the station.

She knew what he wanted, and she wanted it, too. She remembered the warmth of his body against hers, his strong hands pulling her closer, their lips meeting and tongues dancing. She eyed him with lust, imagining their bodies entwining, his strong thighs between hers.

Moments flew by as they walked in the warm summer air, and suddenly they had arrived at her door. Abigail saw in his eyes that his imagination was rioting as much as her own. London grasped both of her hands, not dropping his gaze.

"I won't invite myself in."

"You won't have to."

She pushed the common door open and guided him in.

The pair slid off their shoes in the entryway before Abigail slid her key into the lock on her apartment door.

When they entered, she asked tentatively, "Shall I put on some tea?"

She moved toward the kitchen, but then he reached for her, closing the door with his bare foot and wrapping his arms around her.

"No tea," he muttered into her hair, breathing her scent in deeply.

"Then a tour?"

She leaned into his chest a moment, pressing her cheek to him, before grasping his hand and pulling him directly toward her room, the one and only stop on the tour.

She had no sooner flipped on the light than he reached for her, his fingers curling around her waist and lowering both of them onto the futon. A muscular arm wrapped around her waist and he pressed his lips to hers. Breath escaped her. Her heart pounded and her head spun.

When he released her mouth, she whispered, "Always such urgency."

"Urgent only to be with you," he replied, running fingertips across her cheekbone. "The end will never come urgently."

She read the promise not on his lips but in the shiver across his shoulders. He wanted her as badly as she wanted him, and he certainly was not as good at hiding it.

Under other circumstances Abigail would have hesitated, as she had previously when she found herself tempted by London. She'd think of their working relationship, of her independence, and of his eventual and certain trip back to Maui, away from her.

But that hesitation was suddenly and completely gone, washed away in the memory of a perfect day soaking in his beauty and serenity. Muted by the fire burning in his aqua eyes. By his determined jaw. By the cotton-soft lips. The desire in his voice.

When she ran her hands under his shirt, he immediately reached behind him and pulled it over his head, his golden waves floating down around his face.

His body was even more defined than his clothes had hinted at. Smooth tanned skin stretched tautly over chiseled muscles.

Abigail reached out a hand to touch his chest. Her fingers had hardly made contact when he leaned forward, grabbing her hand and pressing it against his heart. He then pushed her firmly, and as she fell backward, he cradled her head and neck with one large hand so she couldn't have landed any gentler if she'd lain back on the futon on her own.

His mouth came down onto hers, his tongue exploring.

London's fingers found the pearlescent buttons on the side of her skirt, and he flicked them open one at a time, quickly, deftly, eagerly.

Abigail hadn't realized she was holding her breath until London asked, "Are you okay?"

"What?" She breathed in, suddenly feeling lightheaded.

"You weren't breathing. You okay?"

"More than." She breathed in again, reaching around him, her palms flat on his sculpted back, pulling him down again greedily.

Between caresses, between lips, and tongues, and skin, she confirmed, "I want this . . . oh, I want this . . ."

Outside someone played classical guitar, a song she didn't recognize, but the notes floated through the open window. Inside, Abigail and London's bodies danced to the tune.

CHAPTER 7

"Good morning, handsome."

Abigail propped herself up on one elbow on her futon and ran her fingers along London's scruffy jaw line. He opened one eye, the aqua iris piercing in the sunlight pouring in through the windows.

"Geez, woman! Didn't I wear you out last night?" London chuckled and pulled the sheets over his head. "What time is it?"

"It's eight o'clock. And I had a fantastic time last night, thank you very much."

"Then why are you awake? Unless . . ." He peeked out from under the sheet and she could see that he was smiling. "Unless you're ready for a little more something fantastic."

Abigail climbed up onto her knees on the futon, pulling the white sheets up around her nude body while exposing his. She sat back on her heels, tucking the sheet around her bosom and smiling down at the man who lay beside her.

He was stretched out, golden skin gleaming in the morning light, shadowing all the right edges to emphasize his lines.

"As nice as that would be," she said, meaning it in every way as she took in the sight of him, "we have a festival to attend."

"I hadn't heard it called that before, but that's cool."

London grabbed her waist and pulled her back down on the bed, propping himself over her, kissing her cheeks, her neck. He'd just urged the white sheet down to expose her breasts when she swatted at his shoulder.

"You're my date for the festival!"

"Did I agree to that?"

"Not specifically, but I imagine you don't want me to find another date."

"I most certainly do not," he replied, nipping at her collarbones.

"Then let's get showered. You're in for a great time!"

"I sure am."

In one sweeping movement, London pulled the sheet from Abigail's body and lifted her into his arms. Slipping out of the futon, he held her close, kissing any inch of skin he could reach. She moaned, settling into his embrace, allowing herself to be carried down the hall and into the bathroom, and then into the shower.

❧

They were early enough to get seats on the train. Those on the train now were groups of locals and *gaijin* visiting and awaiting the day ahead of them. Most exited at Nagoya Station, and as London and Abigail changed platforms for the train that would take them to the out-lying village, Abigail stopped at the SunRUs.

"Whew," she muttered, motioning London to the newspaper stand.

"Want me to buy it?"

"They don't mind if you look at it here at the stand," she explained, picking up the paper. "You should see the businessmen reading their porn while waiting for trains. But look at this, London. This isn't good."

He came to her side, and she pointed to the headline, paraphrasing.

"Two more English World officials are missing. Yoskikazu Yamamoto and Toru Ito. The CFO and the VP. Still no word on Mr. Inudori, and now these two."

London's shoulders dropped. "Probably went to join the CEO in Bermuda. Hide out until the company goes under."

"They still don't know," she said, skimming the article. "Could be kidnapping. No ransom notes, and no bodies have shown up. But it is still a possibility."

"Have you ever met either of them? Or Inudori?"

"I once sat across from Toru Ito at a corporate dinner. Mr. Ito seemed decent enough. Very nice to me, actually."

"Nice doesn't mean honest. No way have they been kidnapped. Three top execs? They've hit the road."

Abigail sighed. More bad news for the school. More bad news for her teachers. How many would pick up a paper over the weekend . . . and how many would decide not to show up on Monday? How could she blame them?

London wrapped an arm around her waist and pulled her close. She allowed it, dropping the newspaper back on the stand.

"Hey, now. Don't let this ruin the day."

"If they've been kidnapped, that's scary. And if they've abandoned the school, that's bad news, too."

"But we're going to the festival today. And so long as you don't know where the guys are, there isn't anything you can do about it right now. Let's enjoy ourselves."

Abigail rested her head on London's shoulder.

"I'm starting to get really discouraged. How much longer will it be worth fighting for the school?"

He squeezed her, but didn't have an answer.

❧

"It's only a few blocks to where the shrine will depart," Abigail explained as they stepped off the train and onto the platform of the village's tiny outdoor train station. "Even if I hadn't been here before, it would be easy to find simply by following all the townspeople walking to the festival. They're here to celebrate, too."

"Departure shrine?" London asked, a quizzical look on his face as they made their way down the narrow street.

"The shrine is housed at one temple for part of the year, and during this festival, it is carried to another temple to stay for the spring."

When they reached the place, it was unmistakable. Outside the cement *tori* gate hung bright yellow banners with white *kanji* spelling out the name of the harvest festival. The drawing of the goddess' face, bean-shaped and smiling, promised quite a day.

Abigail had been quiet on the train ride, and London had held her close. She appreciated that he wasn't offering solutions. He couldn't have any that would be much help, and what she needed was for him just to be there.

The couple walked through the *tori* gate and gazed at the towering trees surrounding the temple. They immediately caught the eye of everyone there. No one had any qualms about staring at the tall, tanned blond and the curvy African-American woman on his arm. Likewise, this freed Abigail and London to stare back at the scene.

Five townsfolk stood, eyes lowered, toward the center of the temple grounds. Their iridescent robes had underlying hues of violet, green and blue. Gold circle emblems on the fabric blazed in the morning sunlight streaming through the tree branches. Each wore a tall, black felt hat with what looked like a dent in the front. One man held a black wooden flute. He also had a white surgical mask over his nose and mouth.

London nodded in his direction.

"What's with the masks?" he asked Abigail under his breath. "I see people wearing them all over the place. Makes me wonder if I ought to be wearing one, too."

"People are just nervous about getting sick. They don't really take time off work."

Just then another masked participant walked by, an elderly woman leading a group of six other women. Each wore a long, orange cotton robe and, over their hair, a floor-length, white cotton head covering, tied with a string under the chins. Most wrapped the edges around the front of themselves as they chatted with one another.

Just then, the group gathered in close and the mask-wearing nun pulled from her robes a lime green cell phone. She flipped it open, looked down at the screen as she pointed the phone at the group and took a picture.

"There's another example of the beautiful contradiction that is Japan, as I was telling you about yesterday. I sure do love this country," Abigail mused, her mood lightening.

Suddenly, music began and the crowd divided to let through a man on stilts. He wore a red lacquer mask with an angry expression. A white beard, mustache, and hair flowed from the mask and from under the tall and pointy orange, black, and gold hat. He carried a spear in one hand, and his companions, two men in white robes, carried sheathed swords.

"I think it's starting," Abigail said.

"So they'll carry the shrine from this temple up to the temple where it will stay for the season?" London asked.

"That's right."

"Is the festival here, or at the other temple?"

"It kind of reminds me of a small-town parade," Abigail replied, "except that everyone's involved in moving down the street. Then at the other temple there will be something more like a festival, with street food vendors and places to pray and stuff."

"So where's the shrine that they're going to move?"

Abigail scanned the premises before catching sight of it. She motioned for him to follow her and they approached a small glittering gold model temple perched on a polished wood table. Everything about the miniature temple reached for the heavens. Narrow at the bottom and opening wider at the top, it had gold feather-like fingers on the tip of the roof, reaching even further.

"Here it is."

"It's much smaller than I'd expected."

"Small, yes, but it houses a god," she explained. "See the food they put on the shrine? The carrots and green beans and apples? They're offerings."

"Like at the cemetery yesterday. Beer for the ancestors, fruit and veggies for the gods," London said with a smile.

"Well, see those little white porcelain cups on the shrine?"

"Yeah."

"*Sake.*"

Just then, a group of men surrounded the shrine, slipping four slick black poles under the shrine, between it and the table holding it; two poles pointed north and south and two pointed east and west.

London examined the group's blue kimono-style robes. The bright blue was offset by bold red *kanji* on the back, and white and black scarves.

"Are those guys priests?"

"No, they're townsfolk. They'll take turns carrying the shrine."

As if on cue, men grabbed the black poles, two men per pole per side for a total cluster of sixteen townsfolk. One counted off, and then all sixteen lifted the shrine from the table. Another robed man grabbed the table and followed the group as they headed toward the *tori* gate.

More blue-robed men appeared on the scene carrying tall bamboo reeds topped with colored paper fans. It was sudden, the splash of color in the courtyard, and then everyone was following the shrine and the men with the fans.

"Come on!" Abigail urged, taking London by the hand. "I have to warn you, though. People may be serious now, but once the *sake* starts flowing the mood is really going to change."

"You didn't say anything about *sake*."

"I promise you won't be empty-handed for long."

They followed the colorful crowd, and no sooner had they passed through the *tori* gate than a blue-robed man pushed a white paper cup into their hands. He held up a green bottle and didn't wait for them to agree before filling their cups with the clear liquid.

"How much do we pay him?" London asked.

Abigail felt guilty for not having mentioned this before; poor guy must be worried how much this date would cost him.

"Nothing. Some of the money from offerings is saved up to feed people during the festival. If you want street food later, that will cost money."

"*Arigatou gozaimasu.*" She nodded her thanks to the man before raising her cup to London. "Here's to your first festival."

"And here's to us."

The crowed was already pushing them down the street when Abigail took her first sip. The clear, sweet liquid made its way down her throat, burning only momentarily. She coughed, and then another man was topping off her cup before she could take another sip.

"*Arigatou.*"

She turned to see London's cup being refilled, and a beer, Draft One brand, being pushed into his free hand.

"Oh, no thanks. I already have this." He raised his cup. The only response was another man trying to add more *sake* to his cup.

"Don't bother telling them no," Abigail said and laughed.

Her thoughts were brought back to her first festival, before she'd built up her tolerance for *sake*, when she tried discreetly to empty her cup in the bushes, only to have another townsperson peer into her cup and refill it over and over.

Five years gone already. And was this chapter coming to an end? Should she be looking for another job, or keep trying to ride the storm that English World was becoming, regardless of the drama and mystery of it all? When would things get back to the way they used to be?

Of course, they way they used to be didn't include London Crane. And how nice it was to have him around.

"You American?" she heard a man asking London, in broken English.

"Yes, I am."

"Where America?"

"Oh, Maui."

A blank stare.

"Hawaii," he clarified.

"Yes. Why you here?"

"To teach English."

London shot Abigail a glance. Had he thought even mentioning it would bring her back to the news of this morning?

"Take," the blue-robed man commanded of London, holding out a large plastic bag of a dried, stringy meat.

"It's fish jerky," Abigail explained, and she reached into the bag. "Better take it. He's not going to take no for an answer."

London tucked the beer can in the crook of his elbow, laughed and grabbed a handful of jerky with the hand that wasn't holding the *sake*.

They followed the shrine, blue-robed men grabbing their arms from time to time to ask "American?" and "*Sake*?"

London now had two beer cans tucked under his elbow, one paper cup of sake, and another handful of fish jerky when the shrine made a quick stop. One man placed the table underneath it, and two apparently drunk men grabbed London by the elbows.

They took his beer and *sake* and fish jerky, placing it into Abigail's arms, to her surprise. Then they guided London, who kept turning to look over his shoulder at Abigail, to the shrine.

They motioned for him to pick it up, to take their place for a while.

London shrugged at Abigail when he realized he was to take the place of the two drunk men. Abigail admittedly had not seen anything like this before. She was used to special treatment, but an offer to carry the town's shrine? My goodness.

London took it all in stride. He hoisted his end with the rest of them and the group resumed their quick pace down the street.

The *sake* hit Abigail all at once. The street was awhirl with colors; blue robes, green *sake* bottles, bronze beer cans, yellow banners, red flags, rainbow-colored fans. London was in front of her, down the road, carrying a gold shrine. The muscles in his back flexed with his movements. She allowed her eyes to drop to his hips.

She felt drunk already.

And tomorrow was work.

And there were no promises about what her future would hold.

But tonight?

Tonight she'd be with him.

❧

The shrine reached the main temple after a steep climb for the last leg of the road. The blue-robed men had relieved London by that time, for which he admitted to Abigail he was thankful.

"It was as heavy as you'd expect a big gold shrine to be," he laughed, the *sake* slurring his words just the slightest bit. "And that is a steep hill."

"Oh, come on," she teased, also under the influence. "You've got the stamina."

London pulled her close to him, dipped her with a hand on the small of her back, and kissed her full on the lips. The *sake* in her cup spilled on the road.

"I'd rather save my *stamina* for later."

Another man refilled her cup.

❧

The final quarter-mile of road leading to the temple was lined with vendors. Abigail leaned heavily against London to steady herself.

"You're so strong," she purred. Knowing she was drunk, she was careful not to slur her words, but paid no attention to what she said. "You carried the shrine."

"And I'm basically carrying you now," London teased. "Had enough *sake*?"

"You *did* carry me! This morning. Just lifted me up and carried me like it was nothing." Abigail dropped her voice to a conspiratorial level. "You carried me to the shower."

"Do you need something to eat? Or want something?"

"I sure do want something," she flirted. She wasn't so drunk that she had no self-realization, just fewer inhibitions. She hoped she'd remember the day forever, but that the *sake* would censor from her memory the more ridiculous lines she heard tumbling from her lips.

London hadn't caught her double-entendre. He scanned the nearby booths.

"Let's see. You got some French fries, some frozen bananas with all different colors of coating, and then some, what are those? Looks like potatoes, spiral cut, speared and fried. What are those things over there? Tortillas with whipped cream on them?"

Abigail took a glance at the display case. "They're crepes. The display just has them opened up so you can see what's in them."

"Is that a sign error on the display or are they really called Poo Crepes?"

Abigail laughed louder than usual. "Poo Crepes! Look, they wrap them in paper printed with Winnie-the-Pooh characters. Either they wrote it wrong, or the 'h' has been scratched off. I don't want a Poo Crepe!"

London looked into the next booth.

"How about some octopus tentacles drenched in barbeque sauce?"

"I want to see the temple grounds. What time is it? They'll be throwing *mochi* soon."

"Let's get some food in you first. Gotta soak up all that *sake*."

Abigail pulled away from him. "I'm drunk, you know," she announced.

He smiled, but didn't respond.

"I'm pretty drunk," she repeated, lowering her voice so he'd know she was serious.

"I know you are." He grabbed her around the waist, laughing and drawing her close. "I just want to feed you. How about some fries?"

She consented, but the prior concern about him running out of money and leaving began to push through her drunken thoughts. The rational part of her knew that he was just trying to be nice and gentlemanly, but the *sake* made her mind fuzzy, and she felt something akin to annoyance at his assumption that she needed him for anything. She'd come to Japan not knowing the language and made it on her own. And now he was telling her when to eat?

She put a fry in her mouth and the street swayed under her. She laughed, hardly sure she could trust her feet, let alone her thoughts.

Oh, he'd been fun to be with, day and night. Heck, no one could deny that he'd been good in bed. And tonight he'd be fun again.

But she *could* take care of herself. She chomped at the cold fries as she walked ahead of him, swaying, toward the temple.

The banners here were mixed. The yellow banner with the bean-like face was now accompanied by red banners bearing a Rubenesque nude goddess, heavy breasts boasting perky nipples. A lute covered her most private area. Even a harvest goddess, essentially a fertility goddess, had a little modesty.

"There's the shrine." London pointed it out. "So it will stay at this temple for the rest of the year?"

"Yeah. See, people are leaving offerings."

"So where is this *mochi* throwing thing you wanted to go to?"

"It isn't where, but when. And I think we're getting close to when."

Abigail looked at the sun. London followed her gaze into the sky.

"Are you telling time by the sun?" he teased. "Is this another interesting thing you do when you're drunk?"

"First of all, the greasy fries have helped ease the *sake's* effects on me. And second, I'm not telling time so much by the sun, as I am just getting a general feel for the time of day."

"I'm going to buy you a watch. You run multiple schools all throughout Nagoya but you don't even wear a watch."

She cringed. Most girls would enjoy this, being given gifts left and right. But his gut reaction to anything was to buy her something, and that didn't sit right with her. A tea set, French fries, a watch. Did he have no concept of the well running dry, or was he ready to leave?

"Why is how I keep time a problem for you?"

"It isn't a problem. It's just odd."

"You don't wear a watch, either," she pointed out, gesturing toward his naked wrists. Heck, he hardly wore shoes unless they were absolutely necessary.

"I was just offering! I didn't realize you'd be offended by the offer of a gift."

London held his hands up as though he were surrendering.

"But your answer to everything is to buy me something."

She turned her back and looked through the *tori* gate and down the crowded street. Couples and families and friends perused the vendors' booths, buying food and trinkets. Buying each other food and trinkets.

Before she knew it, he was behind her, his arms wrapping around her waist, pulling their bodies together. He nuzzled her hair, buried his face in the back of her neck.

Then he leaned forward and whispered in her ear.

"I know you don't need anyone to take care of you, Abigail. You're strong, independent. But . . ."

His voice dropped, so low and soft that if he hadn't been millimeters away from her ear, she'd not have heard it. He made it sound like a secret.

". . . I'm simply crazy about you. About how you treat those around you. How you care about people. I'm crazy for every moment we spend together, the way you choose your words when we speak, eloquent but not pretentious."

She relaxed in his arms, drew in a breath.

"And I'm crazy about how you feel on my fingertips, on my lips, against my body. Like our bodies are meant to be next to one another. I keep offering you things. It's what I know how to do, but it obviously isn't what you want."

"Not things," she muttered, turning her head to look into his face.

"Can I dare to hope what you'd prefer I offer?"

"Only yourself."

He leaned into her, the busy festival around them now just a swirl of colors, as though only they mattered. Only this moment.

"I can give you that."

His body was so firm against hers, and she melted into it.

"*Mochi*-throwing . . . ," she muttered. "The priests throw rock-hard balls of *mochi*—about the size of soft-balls—at the crowd to catch. You cook it at home and it's okay. The fun is trying to catch it."

"Okay . . ."

"Now that you know all about *mochi*-throwing, there's no use in waiting around a while for it to happen."

He caught her drift, turned her to face him, leaned down and kissed her mouth airily.

"London," she said into his lips. "Now that you know all about it, we might as well go."

"To?"

"To my apartment."

❧

Abigail had just said goodbye, a long goodbye that led back into the apartment and down onto the kitchen floor before London finally shuffled back down the street toward the train station. She pulled on her light, kimono-style robe.

When her cell phone rang she shivered, thinking it might be him. As much as she needed a few hours to herself to get a shower, get prepared for classes tomorrow, and get some shut-eye, she couldn't help hoping it was him. Maybe he'd missed the last train because of their long goodbye and now needed a place to sleep. As though they'd sleep much.

The picture that popped up on the cell phone screen, though, was the strawberry blonde with perfect teeth.

"I know it's late," Savannah said as soon as Abigail flipped open the phone.

"Hello to you, too."

"I'm sorry, I was hoping I'd catch you awake."

"I'm still hours from sleep," she answered, thinking she couldn't possibly sleep just now, not after the night she'd had, regardless of how tired her body felt.

"I just wanted to ask if you've gotten the English World offer?" Savannah's voice was uncharacteristically tense.

"Offer?"

"Remember?" Her voice dropped to a whisper. "They sent me an offer to go away for a while. Did they send you one, Abby?"

"Oh, no, they never did. Is everything okay?"

Savannah sighed, and when she spoke again she was no longer whispering, and no longer sounded quite so concerned.

"Okay. I think that's a good sign. Did you see the news today—"

"About Yoskikazu Yamamoto and Toru Ito? Yeah. Bad news all around."

"I know they might have just run off. But remember, we met Toru Ito at that dinner? He didn't seem like a corrupt executive. He was younger, and he was really into your ideas about pedagogy. I thought he cared about what we were doing as a company."

"I had sort of forgotten about that dinner until I saw his name today. He was so nice to me, and very passionate about education."

"Yeah, and I'd forgotten about the dinner, too, until today. So it got me thinking, what if they were kidnapped, too? I'm thinking . . . well, I'm thinking of taking English World up on their offer. I'm going to have to close the school here in a week or two anyway. I might as well get them to pay for me to go home."

"Is the offer to be sent home?"

"Well, sent somewhere safe."

"Does it say you can come back?"

"Yeah, it's just temporary. They'll pay for me to come back, too. I never replied to the original letter, so hopefully I still can."

Abigail leaned back. "Why not? I mean, I doubt you're in any danger. No administrative heads have gone missing. Just the head honchos. We're just as much victims as anyone else. But why not get a free trip home, or a free trip somewhere safe, if the school's going to close anyway?"

Savannah sighed again. "I'm not as nervous, I have to say. I just hate giving up on the school."

"If English World pulls it together, you'll come back to your position. If they don't . . . well, at least you did your best and probably have a free ticket home."

"I'm going to think about it this week, but I'll probably take them up on it. Can I call you later this week to let you know for sure? And maybe plan a day or two in Nagoya? I'd really like to see you again before I go."

"I'd love that," Abigail said with a smile, wondering if it would be too soon to introduce her to London.

"On to a better subject," Savannah announced, her voice chipper. "I feel better about the whole thing knowing it means I get to spend some time with my favorite *gaijin*!"

Abigail knew this bubbly voice, and now wondered how long sadness had been behind it without anyone knowing.

"What are you doing with your free time, Abby?"

"Umm . . . ," she stalled, carrying her phone to the bedroom and settling down on her futon.

"Sounds like something *interesting*," Savannah cooed. "Maybe even a man in Abigail Dennis's life. Finally. A good man, I mean. Not one that flashes her on the street."

It was admittedly hot outside, her body still especially warm from the heights and depths London had taken her to. Places she'd not known possible.

"You guessed it," she admitted.

"So . . . who is he?"

"A new teacher—"

"New?"

"That's right . . . the schmucks can't pay the teachers they have and they're still hiring more. But anyway, he's a teacher here in Nagoya."

"Where's he from?"

This was one of the forefront questions when it came to any teacher. To any *gaijin,* for that matter.

"Maui."

"Nice! I love Maui!"

"I haven't been. When did you go?"

"For my brother's wedding. Remember when I took my vacation during the summer a year or so ago instead of during the new year holiday?"

"Oh, yeah. You said it was a really nice wedding, I remember."

"The hotel was really nice, anyway. Very posh. I couldn't even afford to stay there . . . just showed up for the wedding and then went back to my *affordable* hotel."

"It's funny—his family has a little hotel in Maui. Maybe you stayed at his place."

"What's it called?"

Abigail scanned her memory. How could she not know the answer to that? She was sleeping with a guy whose family owned a hotel and she didn't even know the name of it?

"I guess I never asked. His name is Crane, if that rings a bell."

Silence.

"Savannah? You there?"

"Did you say his name is London Crane?"

"Yeah. Oh, wait, no. I didn't. I just said his name is Crane. How do you know his first name?"

More silence.

"Hello? Savannah?"

"Sorry. Are you kidding me? This man, this *teacher* is the same London Crane from the hotels?"

Abigail stood up and moved to the open screen of the window, an attempt to cool down. "I assumed it was only one hotel that his family owned."

"Well, his family owns several. His sisters, I mean. I think Sofia Crane owns all of their hotels on the East Coast of the U.S. Yasna Crane owns the Asia-based hotels. And what is the third sister's name? Oh, Nichol Crane. She owns the ones in Canada, Mexico and a few in South America. London Crane owns the hotels on the West Coast of the U.S., the ones in Hawaii, and the ones in Europe. And I *think* he's recently opened one in Dubai."

"How could I not know about this chain of hotels?"

"If you dropped a cool thousand on your hotel rooms, you'd know about them." Savannah laughed. "Not that I do that. But my brother's wedding was at The C in Maui. London Crane owns that one. Not the crappy one I stayed at."

"The C? I know that name. But I don't think we're talking about the same London Crane."

"Maybe not. But he did personally run the one in Maui. I never spoke to him, but I did see him walking through the foyer one day. I thought he was just a guest since he was so dressed down. He was wearing board shorts and a tank top. The only reason I noticed him at all was that he was smokin' hot and I asked the bellhop if he was a movie star. My God, those arms."

Abigail conceded to herself that that sounded like London. In looks, anyhow.

"The bellhop told me who he was. Said he ran the place, but did some kind of guest tours, too. That's why he was in shorts."

"Kayak tours," Abigail blurted out before she could stop herself.

"That's it!"

The pair became quiet, and Abigail touched the window screen, trying to picture Hibino station. Where around there would London be staying? She'd simply pictured an apartment not unlike her own. She hadn't been there, though, and she hadn't asked him about it. She'd assumed he was a starving teacher. She'd wanted him to save his money and not buy her French fries or a watch.

"You're dating London Crane from The C line of hotels. And he never told you."

Abigail breathed in.

"Does it change how you see him?"

Abigail knew Savannah knew her. Knew that Abigail wouldn't see London's wealth or prestige. She'd see that he hadn't been up front.

"He never lied about it," she admitted, both to her friend and to herself. "I just never prodded for details."

He hadn't lied. He'd told her he managed a hotel and led kayak tours. He'd been nothing if not honest.

To her surprise, once she assured herself he'd been as trustworthy as she'd been trusting, she realized the news didn't change how she saw him at all.

Granted, it would make for an interesting conversation on Monday.

CHAPTER 8

"I almost turned around and came back to your place last night," London announced as he shut the office door behind him.

There'd been fewer people than ever at the Monday staff meeting, but London had smiled at her, sharing their secret. Of course, he didn't know how many of his secrets she now knew.

"Mmm?" she muttered, looking in the locker for her books.

London made it to her in three paces, wrapping his arms loosely around her waist and nuzzling her neck. She leaned her head back, relaxing her body into his.

"Would you have wanted me to come back?"

She turned in his arms to face him, took his face in her hands and planted a firm kiss on his lips.

"I wanted you to. But in hindsight, it was a *productive* night and so it is probably better you didn't."

"Since you were so productive last night, I think you ought to take it easy tonight. Go to bed early."

Abigail hadn't decided on the best way to tell London she knew much more about him this morning than she had the last time he had gathered her into his arms, just twelve hours ago. She didn't want to sound accusatory— he hadn't done anything wrong, after all. And she really didn't want to sound glad because he might see that as her reaction to his wealth, and not as relief at the possibility of him sticking around.

Perhaps the best thing to do was to wait it out. Let him tell her.

"Are you suggesting I stay home? Or are you inviting me to your apartment?"

Abigail looked up at him coyly, flirting.

"I don't have an apartment, actually. I'm living in a hotel. A cold, impersonal hotel."

Was there a C Hotel off Hibino station? Abigail hadn't noticed. She hadn't paid attention prior to his arrival because it wasn't like she could afford to stay someplace like that, even in the fat years.

London recognized in her eyes that she was mulling something over, but his guess about what it was happened to be wrong.

"Before you ask if it's *wise* for me to stay at a hotel while I don't have money coming in from English World—"

"I wasn't going to even mention it."

Abigail thought he might answer, *For once*, but he didn't. His eyes smiled, and finally, after a quiet moment, he flashed his crooked grin.

"You weren't going to mention it. And I didn't even need to offer to show you my bank statements."

They both laughed, and Abigail pried herself free to finish grabbing books from her locker. "So your place then?"

"I told you; it's cold. Impersonal."

"Hotels aren't that bad," she countered.

Did he really feel this way? Or was he at a competing hotel and didn't like the environment? Was he just trying to keep her from knowing that he was living in a neat little room at one of the priciest hotel chains in the world, a chain owned by his family? Would people say "*Konnichiwa*, Mr. Crane" when he walked through the doors? Hadn't Savannah mentioned one of his sisters owned hotels in Asia?

"I like your place," he said, grabbing her books from her arms when she turned around again. It was like high school. Except no one in high school had carried her books. Students had given that up by the time she was in high school. Had they ever done it, or was it just in the movies?

London did it now. Gathered up her books and tucked them under an arm.

"My apartment is all right, but it isn't anything special."

"It's cozy," he replied, grasping her hand with his free hand. "I like it a lot. I especially like your futon."

She swatted his shoulder. "Fine, then. But I don't think hotels are impersonal."

"Believe me," he muttered, "they are."

❧

Abigail had hoped Saori's workload would have eased up by now. Exams had been completed and the students deserved a break. Meaning English World deserved a break. Meaning Saori and the teachers deserved a break.

But Saori seemed frazzled. A group of parents around the reception desk were arguing in Japanese when Abigail entered after her classes. Abigail noticed dark circles under Saori's eyes, and her usually neat appearance was edging toward ragged.

"English World is closed for the night," Abigail announced to the parents. She propped the door open behind her and crossed her forearms to form an X. Then she motioned the parents toward the door.

There was copious grumbling that she was sure they thought she couldn't translate, but finally the parents made their way out. Abigail locked the door lest students filter in after their classes to demand better schedules than Saori could offer.

"Saori," she broached the subject as delicately as she could, setting her books on the reception desk, "you seem very tired. Do you need a day off?"

Even as she said it, and even as she hoped Saori would take her up on it, she wondered how in the world she'd cover for teachers *and* reception-administration, even for a day. She'd just have to close the front door. Go to classes and hold off on any scheduling until later.

"No," was the quiet reply. "I do not need a day off of work. I am fine."

"I know you do more than your fair share during the workday. You're not working late, are you?"

"I am just worried about things." She sighed. "I will need to take a second job soon. I must bring some money to my home. My parents do not understand why I work and not get paid."

"If you need to resign," Abigail cringed even as she offered it, "I understand."

"No, I do not resign. English World will pay us eventually, I think."

Abigail managed a slight smile, wondering if Saori believed this, or if she were testing the waters to find out if Abigail herself believed it any longer.

"Well, it's hard to know now. I'm sure you've seen in the news that two more people from headquarters are missing."

"I did read that, yes."

"It isn't looking good."

"I suppose it is not."

Abigail tapped her fingers on the desk. "I think it's time for you to leave for the night. I can close up. You've seemed to do it every night lately."

Saori looked at her computer screen, then down at the calendar book on her desk. "I think I should finish. Then I can close up."

Abigail got a bad feeling that Saori really might have been working late and not marking her time. It wouldn't be out of character, and someone less invested in her staff might brush it off since no one was getting paid anyway. But she didn't like it.

"I'll wait for you. Just come get me in my office when you're done and we can walk to Nagoya Station together."

And so that Saori couldn't argue, Abigail scooped up her books and made her way down the short hall to her office. She hoped it wouldn't be long, and she pulled out her phone to send a quick text to London just in case.

Waiting for Saori, she wrote. *Will call when I leave.*

As her finger pressed the send button, a shiver ran through her. It wouldn't be long before her fingers would be tracing the distinct lines of London's body. Would it feel different, knowing a secret he didn't know she knew? Would he be able to tell she was holding something back?

This level of lust was so unlike her, she realized. It grew exponentially each time.

Her phone chimed.

I've been thinking . . . , he'd texted in reply.

As she read she thought of how little they'd texted each other. She was surprised that he texted the way one might email, without the usual terseness that was the signature of the text message format.

. . . and I would like you to come to my hotel room. I hope it won't change anything. I still like your place better.

There was another chime and she read, *I am off Hibino, four blocks away at The C Hotel Nagoya. I'll leave a message at Reception that I'm expecting you. Until then, London.*

Abigail slipped her phone into her purse on the desk. There it was then. She didn't need to tell him anything, didn't even need to pry it out of him. He was offering the truth to her, just like that.

"Now I have to pretend like I'm surprised."

It was ridiculous that she had to think about this petty stuff right now. Her school was going under. Her staff would soon be unemployed. And her superiors were either on the lam or tied up in someone's basement.

She *wouldn't* worry about it, she decided. She'd just tell him the truth . . . he trusted her and valued trust. Things were too serious right now for her to have the luxury of flirty games.

She was so used to second-guessing the intentions of men around her. And so used to the knowledge that her community was a fleeting one. And now she'd learned that London might have the resources to stay a while. And now he was willing to be open and honest with her. A weight was lifting from Abigail's shoulders.

Saori popped her head around the corner of Abigail's office without a sound. If she'd not been facing the door, Abigail wouldn't have noticed she was there at all.

"Oh, hi Saori. Are you ready to go?"

"I do have more to do here," she protested, "but if you insist I do not work late, I can also go now."

Abigail laid a hand on Saori's arm. "I insist."

Together they walked to Nagoya Station. Saori obviously had work on her mind, so Abigail made an attempt to lighten the mood as they walked.

"Have you seen any of those Meiji Strawberry bars around lately?"

"The ones with chocolate?"

"No, just the plain strawberry ones. In the red foil wrappers."

"I have not," she said, her mind obviously elsewhere.

"I used to get them all the time and when things started getting tight, I cut back. Now I can't find them anywhere."

"I think they were . . . what is it called? . . . *limited edition*. You may be able to find them on the internet."

The pair walked further down the sidewalk, before turning into the station. Abigail could have found her way between the station and school in her sleep.

"Abigail, thank you for your concern for me," Saori said suddenly. "I appreciate that you care enough to think of me. Sometimes the teachers forget about me, probably because I am local. Or maybe because I am not a teacher. But I appreciate that you think of me, and that you do not want me to be stressed."

"Of course. And as I said before, if you need to find a different job, I understand. I appreciate all you've done."

"I will try to stay with English World. But it all depends."

Abigail looked at the enormous bronze clock in the inside courtyard, the main meeting place for anyone catching someone else at Nagoya Station. In fact, most of her teachers were trying to get independent one-on-one tutoring gigs on the side, and they often used this clock as the place to meet their students. Then they'd find a café to sit in and make a few bucks just giving someone a chance to practice conversational English.

"My train will be here soon," Saori announced, looking at the clock. "I will see you tomorrow morning. Goodbye, Abigail."

"Good night."

And with that, Saori disappeared into the crowd of businessmen and women. Abigail decided to stop in the

SunRUs to search for some Meiji Strawberry. What a treat it would be if she could share it with London.

No Meiji Strawberry in the little convenience store. She looked at her watch. Yes, there was time to peek into Tokyu Hands just in case. The five-story department store had everything else, after all, from electronics and role-playing clothing to science equipment and craft supplies.

She rode the escalator, her mind focused on Meiji Strawberry and London. What an odd turn her life had taken. Just when things seemed darkest, and just when things *were* darkest, this light appeared to make life beautiful again. Not easy, but lovely nonetheless.

The televisions in the electronics section were all on the same channel as she walked by them. It was in Japanese, but just as she was about to pass the last television screen, the picture that flashed up caught her eye.

There were three rectangular frames, two holding English World staff photographs and one blank with the kanji for something to the effect of "photo not yet available." She recognized the first two, to her rising horror, as Richard Mulrooney and Amy Hart, the administrative heads of English World Tokyo and English World Kyoto.

She whipped back to the screen, paying close attention to the words spoken. Richard and Amy were missing, just like the others. It was the first time staff that were not from headquarters had disappeared. The news reported no signs of struggle. In fact, Amy's roommate even reported her carry-on luggage missing, along with a week's worth of clothes and prescription medications.

Abigail's mind snapped back to Savannah's offer from English World. Could that be all these "missing persons" were? Secretive offers from English World to lay low for a while, just in case someone was angry with them?

That was it, she decided. She'd figured it out, and now the authorities ought to know, too. It was wrong that whoever at English World—the board maybe—that was making these offers weren't telling the police about them. Then again, maybe they had told the police, and not the media. After all, the idea was to let a few people slip out of the country briefly until the mess cleared.

Abigail flipped her cell phone open and chose Savannah's smiling face out of a small group of hovering pictures. She dialed her number in Osaka.

Abigail didn't have a letter, but Savannah did. She planned to suggest that Savannah take it to the authorities. Either that, or they could do it together when Savannah came. She could still take the offer, but at least the police would know that the missing people had likely left of their own accord.

The phone rang four times and then voicemail picked up. Savannah had a smart voicemail, Abigail always thought when she called. The message spoke once in English and once in Japanese; Savannah's fluency in Japanese rivaled Abigail's and she thus had no problem either recording the greeting or accepting voicemail in either language.

At the tone, Abigail turned away from the television sets.

"Hey Savannah, it's me. I just saw that Amy Hart and Richard Mulrooney from Tokyo and Kyoto are missing, but Amy took luggage with her. I'm guessing they got the same offer as you did, and I think the police should know in case they don't already. What do you think? If you don't have time, we can see the police when you come over. By the way, I'm really looking forward to seeing you. It's been too long. We're a half hour apart by *Shinkansen* and we still don't get together often enough. I can't wait. Okay, call me."

CHAPTER 9

Though her search for a Meiji Strawberry bar at Tokyo Hands had been thwarted by the news report, Abigail felt relief at the likelihood that her two missing colleagues were okay, on their way home for a few weeks. Or . . . her three colleagues. Richard Mulrooney and Amy Hart and "photo not available."

She found an empty seat in the train between a man wearing a surgical mask and one half of a pair of teenage girls pouring over a magazine featuring the members of a Japanese pop band on the cover.

Her mind turned first to Savannah. How would they spend their last days together? Would she come back to Japan after the English World problems were resolved? Abigail thought of the many weekends she'd sat around reading or temple-hopping alone or milling through Tokyu Hands when she could have been hanging out with her friend. It had been so easy to assume she had all the time in the world.

In her peripheral vision, Abigail noticed the man in the mask staring at her blatantly. Geez, this was getting old.

She turned to look directly back at him and made eye contact. She saw a leering expression in his eyes, though his mouth was covered by the mask. Abigail shook her

head *no* and crossed her forearms before turning away
from him. He'd gotten the picture, and she could see out
of the corner of her eye that he had returned to reading
the advertisements hanging on the wall and from the
ceiling.

Her thoughts switched to London. She wouldn't
make the same mistake as she had with her friends. She'd
appreciate the time she could spend with him.

Her stomach dropped. What should she expect from
The C Hotel Nagoya? Hibino station was fast
approaching, and it would be only a short walk to the
hotel and to London. She wondered if he was also worrying about what she'd say and how she'd react.

My goodness, she thought, *I feel like a schoolgirl.*

She peered over at the teeny-boppers in their modest
blouses and short skirts giggling and chatting over their
magazine. She caught the name of a popular singer,
Yukio, a hit with the girls. Only a month or two ago,
she'd have chuckled to herself, thinking how sweet and
innocent and young they were. And now, inside, she felt
the exact same way as she got closer and closer to The C.

Only, *they've got a crush*, she told herself with a
smirk, and *I'm on my way to London's arms*.

❧

At Hibino station she exited the train, went through
the turnstile, and then exited the building. She looked
left and right, wondering how she'd find the hotel, considered going into the nearby SunRUs to ask the clerk.

But when she turned around she saw looming over the station a mirror-windowed high-rise with a single lighted letter in bold script perched on the roof: *C*.

"I suppose it's safe to assume that's it," she announced with a chuckle, drawing glances from those filtering out around her. She circled around to the back of the station building and headed toward the monstrosity.

It was only four blocks and then she was staring at the circular driveway, the cars driving up to the mirrored sets of double-doors, valets taking luxury cars from wealthy visitors, chauffeurs assisting even wealthier visitors before nodding and driving the cars away themselves.

A black sedan pulled up, and to Abigail's surprise, out stepped Yukio. At least, she thought it was him. His characteristic hair, usually worn long and shaggy or gelled and wild, was pushed under a pageboy cap. Dressed down in jeans and a t-shirt, his eyes were hidden behind tortoise-shell sunglasses.

Abigail assumed he was trying to hide his identity. Perhaps he'd casually grab an overnight bag and nod to his driver, wave off the attendants, walk in alone and give a false name. When a group of girls pushed past Abigail, she almost felt sorry Yukio couldn't have a moment's peace.

And then it was clear. He didn't want a moment's peace. He flashed a smile as the girls rushed up, and several bodyguards stepped menacingly from the car to surround him. He smiled again, lifted his chin—Abigail half-expected him to say " 'sup"—and stood posed for a moment while cell phones snapped pictures.

Attendants surrounded his car, loading their brass pushcarts with endless pieces of his black leather luggage set before heading into the hotel. Yukio took a step, his bodyguards following him, and posed again, looking back over his shoulder.

"Oh, how casual and debonair you are," she muttered, but couldn't help the smile playing across her lips. Those girls in the train would have loved to be here.

Suddenly he was gone. A quick sweep indoors, the girls held back, swooning but respectful.

Abigail made her way to the mirrored doors, acutely aware of how suspect she might look walking in off the street, following after Japan's biggest heartthrob. She straightened her crisp white button-down shirt; the gray pin-stripes running the length of the shirt flattered her curves. She peered at her gray slacks. The cuffs held their shape, and her cute white flats weren't scuffed, even with the walk.

To her surprise, the doormen opened the doors without a second glance. Evidently she looked as though she belonged here, even without the high-end clothes and Coach bag. Then again, maybe she just didn't look like a star-struck teeny-bopper.

"Thanks," she said with a nod to the doorman, who caught her eye, as though surprised that she noticed him, let alone spoke to him.

"You are welcome, madame. Have a nice evening."

His English was impeccable.

"You too," she replied, again surprising him. And then, "Wow . . ." as she stepped into the lobby.

It could have been a blank sheet of paper with furniture drawn onto it, but not colored in. The white rug at the entryway led to the wide open stone floor. The usual characteristic streaking in most marble was almost non-existent in this white marble floor, which was more marble sheets than tiles. How had the stone-cutters found so many flawless sections of marble without cutting it out in little perfect pieces? The grout was equally white, untouched by earth . . . or cleaned constantly.

The walls were blank, stark, with a tall, narrow window every few feet. The street level view was nothing to boast about, and the architecture seemed to usher in enough light to keep spirits high, but enough view to make one feel pleasant about being inside. No photographs were hung, no paintings.

Pairs of white buttery leather sofas faced each other in several spaces near the walls, spotless glass coffee tables dividing them. Even the coasters atop the coffee tables were wispy sheets of glass.

In a photograph with the wrong exposure, the lobby might have looked bare except for one attribute, the one thing that really caught Abigail's eye and held it.

A wide, shallow fountain in the center of the lobby rose almost organically from the marble flooring. Nothing about the fountain was sharp, nothing about the fountain was simplistic. The basin sat only a couple feet tall, and the wide edge encouraged one to sit down. In the middle, many parts of a winding, sweeping sculpture climbed up itself like vines in jewel tones: jade and turquoise and plum and midnight blue. Water drizzled from every crevice and over every crevice, right into the pool. The pool was tiled with a silver, mirror-like flooring so that it reflected the jewel tones of the sculpture.

Abigail moved toward the fountain. It was the only thing with much life in this hotel. She dipped a finger into the cool clear water.

What had London said about hotels? Cold and impersonal? Of course that depended on the hotel. And other than this fantastic, artistic fountain, she had to agree that her apartment, for all its small size and age, was more welcoming.

London.

Abigail sighed and eyed the reception desk. Along the back wall there were no windows, no sofas, no coffee tables. Instead, along the length of the back wall ran a chest-high white bar to serve as a reception desk. There were three reception attendants for each guest, and the guest check-in points were few and far between.

The rich and famous don't even want to talk to one another, Abigail thought as she watched a threesome of pretty attendants check in an older businessman and his elegantly poised wife. One attendant created magnetic keycards, one arranged for their luggage to be brought up, and one handled the paperwork and financial side of the transaction.

She walked up to the nearest trio without a guest.

"*Irasshaimase.*"

"Hello," she replied with a warm smile. "I'm here to see London Crane."

One girl eyed her suspiciously. "Is Mr. Crane expecting you?"

"He is. My name is Abigail Dennis."

Suddenly, from a doorway she hadn't even noticed, since it was cut into the white wall with a white wall behind it, appeared a tanned blonde woman. She was curvy, with padded hips and breasts and legs and arms. She wore her hair long, curly without having been permed, with a white orchid behind one ear.

"Did you say you're Abigail?" she asked.

"Yes. I'm here to see London Crane."

She spoke to the attendants quickly, in Japanese, and they moved aside to let the woman through.

"I'll take you up there myself. You haven't brought anything?"

"Anything?"

"Luggage?"

"No, I'm just stopping in for a few hours."

The woman chuckled softly. "Poor boy. He'll be sorry to hear that."

She led Abigail to a glass elevator, scanned a keycard and pressed the button for Penthouse 2.

"I'm Yasna Crane," she said then, extending a hand. "London's my little brother. And this is my hotel."

The top floor of The C Nagoya was divided into three penthouses, Yasna explained on the way up. She herself was in Penthouse 1 this week, though she explained that if she'd known Yukio would be showing up today, she'd have chosen Penthouse 3.

"Not that he'll be dissatisfied," she said. "The penthouses are basically the same layout with different décor. But many of our patrons feel it is a matter of *class*, which floor you get for the main rooms, and which number you get for the penthouse rooms."

The doors finally opened to a spacious lobby. An attendant rushed up, looking for luggage or shopping bags or something he could assist with.

"Just visiting my brother," Yasna explained with a nod, waving him off.

They passed a small desk with security who didn't dare ask the hotel owner for her keycard, and Abigail noticed several soft leather chairs facing a fireplace. A bartender stood at alert at a small bar in the corner, though no one was around to order.

"Here we are. Stand to the side of the peephole. I want this to be a surprise. He asked me to tell reception to call him when you got here, and not lead you right up. I can't imagine why. But I don't get a lot of chances to trick or tease London anymore, so I couldn't miss this one."

Yasna knocked, squared her shoulders, and winked at Abigail.

There was a shuffle, a pause, and then the door flew wide open.

"Hey, Yaz!"

He didn't step out, and so he didn't see Abigail, Yasna stepped slightly in for the hug. "How's The C Nagoya's P2 suiting you, baby brother?"

"The C Nagoya's P2 is simply spectacular, though I must say we have different decorating tastes."

"Or our hotel decorators have different tastes."

"Yeah, I guess that's it. Anyway, I hate to impose, take up prime real estate here. I wish you'd just let me find a little apartment—"

"Nonsense. How could you be living on the doorstep of one of my loveliest hotels and not be staying in it?"

Abigail heard London laugh, and then there was a pause.

"Any sight of Abigail?" he asked tentatively, as though he thought his big sister would tease him about it.

"You're receiving her dressed like *that*?"

"Come on now, I can dress up quickly. But any word from her? I told you and the attendants on duty she'd be coming and to call me."

"I . . . don't remember that, London."

Abigail held her breath.

"I told you, and everyone downstairs."

"I remember they turned someone away earlier. I didn't hear the conversation, but it was a woman who came in directly after Yukio and they thought she was a groupie."

"What? That better not have been Abigail, Yaz!"

"What does she look like again?"

"She's beautiful, simply beautiful. Casual, but holds herself confidently, you know. Her hair is short and sort of curly. Puts it back in one of those hair things mostly. A headband, I guess you'd call it. She's African-American, and she has a big smile, a huge smile actually. She has this cute thing where she touches the back of her neck if she's nervous about something."

Abigail straightened up. Had she not yet broken that habit? She checked herself, and indeed her palm was resting on the back of her neck. She dropped her hand to her side, chuckling to herself, as Yasna stepped out of Penthouse 2.

"Well, I'll go check downstairs."

"Please. Call me if they sent her away and I'll call her mobile phone. I want to go down to meet her if she's here. I have to explain some things before she comes up here—"

"Oh!" Yasna exclaimed dramatically, grasping Abigail's right hand. "You match London's description."

She urged Abigail into London's line of sight.

He was shocked to see her, but it was only a half-second before a crooked grin spread across his lips.

"Hey now, what are you girls playing at?" And he scooped Abigail into his arms. "I take it you've already met my malicious big sister."

"Don't call me big," Yasna retorted as she began to move back toward the elevator.

London popped his head out the door to call after her.

"You're here a couple more days, so you better watch out. I'll pay you back for that trick."

London moved back into the room and shut the door after himself.

"Well, well, well. And you were in on it, too."

Abigail held up her hands and smiled. "I just stood there and let it happen."

"Sins of omission," he countered, pulling her into his arms. "Maybe we're even, then, since I know I didn't tell you the extent of my job in the hospitality business."

"*Extent* is right."

"Mad at me?" He leaned down, his face close to hers, and she could smell the crisp scent of mint toothpaste on his breath.

"No. You didn't lie. You just gave me enough information to let me make my own assumptions."

"Are you at least confident now that I won't go broke and run for home just because English World isn't paying me?"

"I know I won't protest next time you want to pay for the octopus balls!"

Abigail laughed at her own joke, and his mouth came over hers, swallowing the sound.

She realized from the force of his lips on hers that she wasn't going to get a tour of the place right away. And even though London had planned to dress up more for her, that plan had gone by the wayside now. The black silk boxers and tank top would have to do. For now, at least, if the growing pressure against the fabric was any indication. She slid her hands down his chest, over the thin, fitted black tank top that hugged every line of him.

Her mind flashed to his *Slow Hand Jam* shirt, and the tank top won out for flattering him simply because it laid bare his delicious collar bones and knotted arms.

London grabbed her hips with strong hands, pulling her against him. Her hands flew to his hair, fingers entwining the blond curls and urging his face down again to hers. Their lips met this time with such force that she felt a dull ache, but she pulled him closer still. His tongue danced around hers.

He took a step toward her, forcing her back. Another step and another, until she was against the blank white wall of the foyer. Her hands explored his hard chest, pushed him back just enough to make space for his hands to reach the clasp of her slacks. Unfastening them with a flick of the wrist, he pulled them down with a tug, exposing her caramel thighs.

He reached between them, stroking and exploring, all the while pulling her body against his, urging them closer and closer, as though any space at all between their bodies was too much space. Abigail threw her head back, moaning. His fingers continued to dance as he drew her panties down, down to the floor. She found herself melting into his touch. Melting.

His mouth found the hollow in her throat, his tongue spelled unknown letters. She yanked at his shirt, pulling it over his head clumsily and he undid the buttons on her shirt. Greedily.

"Abigail," he muttered as she stroked him through his boxers.

With a yank she had them down, and with a flash of movement his hands were at her waist and hips, lifting her into the air and then down onto him.

A guttural sound rose from her throat as he entered her. He had to push her back against the wall to sink himself completely inside her. They moved then, no words spoken besides primal chokes of sound between their lips. Her hands entwined in his hair, his hands guided her hips.

When the tip of ecstasy cascaded into full-scale rapture, they collapsed to the tile floor, wrapped up in one another's arms.

❧

Abigail stepped out of the shower. London followed, grabbing an enormous, fluffy bathrobe from the rack beside them and wrapping it around her.

He wrapped a towel around his waist and kissed her on her shoulder where a triangle of skin was exposed where the robe had fallen open.

"Want some dinner? I have got to eat something."

"Dinner sounds good, as long as we don't have to go out for it."

"We'll order in," he said and reached for a cordless phone. "Shall I order? I know the food here like the back of my hand after the past few weeks."

"Sure. Just get a lot of food. I'm ravenous."

London ordered as Abigail inspected her surroundings. The penthouse's living room was white walls and glass. It had one enormous picture on each of the four walls—a clear glass frame, an expanse of white matting, and an eight-by-ten-inch black and white photograph off-center in each frame. A photo of cherry blossoms in one, a sacred pool outside a temple in another, a far-off view of Nagoya Castle, and finally the jagged paper hangings at a Shinto shrine. In the center of the room, a round glass cafe table stood between two buttery leather chairs.

"Not much going on when it comes to the color wheel, is there?" she asked London when he hung up the phone.

"Yaz says it looks classy. And to be honest, it isn't far off from the styles in most high-end hotels here, from what I hear."

"And is your hotel modern and minimalist, too?"

London made his way across the room and wrapped his arms around her waist; she draped hers over his bare shoulders.

"What do you think?"

"I think . . . not if you had any say in the decor."

"You think correct. In the hotel I lived at in Maui, The C Kanapaali, everything is very open to the outdoors. We have tropical plants growing in the open foyer and streams and bridges around the property. And a private beach."

"And your other hotels?"

London raised an eyebrow. "How much did Yaz tell you?"

"Not much."

London first led her to the table and chairs, but reconsidered and led her into the massive bedroom, where the king-sized bed was soft and inviting. They fell onto it, lying on their backs next to one another, Abigail's robe falling open around her shoulders.

"I own a few, to be honest, Abigail. Grew up in a hotel family, and it's just sort of weird to explain. When each of my sisters and I turned eighteen, a hotel was transferred from our parents to our names. It was their way of trying to get us into the business. We'd have to either manage the thing, connect with the current manager to arrange what was needed from us, or figure out how to sell a high-end hotel."

"Was the one in Maui your first?"

"Yeah. My folks preferred we liaise with the hotel managers, but I wanted to do some work there, which is how I started doing kayak tours. Then each year after that they transferred another hotel. For ten years. We each got a territory; they didn't outright say we ought to stay out of the business of competing with one another, but we all think that's why they did it."

"So you have ten hotels?"

"I do. My sisters were a little more entrepreneurial than I was and they've expanded. I've stuck with the ten, Maui, Kauai, Los Angeles, 'Frisco, to name a few. And obviously I got tired of it even with just those."

"I thought you said you left because you were giving the job to the other tour guide." Abigail wondered if he had been untruthful after all.

London rolled over onto his side facing her, and propped his head up on a bent elbow.

"That was true. I wouldn't have left otherwise. But I came here to teach because I wanted something altogether different. I could've just gone to any one of the other hotels. Or could have lived at the one in Kanapaali and left the work to the managers. But if I wasn't going to do a job I loved, then I wanted a change."

Abigail continued staring at the ceiling. "I'm glad you came—"

Just then there was a knock at the door.

London sat up and stretched his arms over his head. "That was quick. And I ordered some really decadent stuff, too."

He made his way to the door and Abigail rolled onto her stomach, resting her chin on her folded hands and looking out the open curtains onto the city she loved so much. If the view was nothing to write home about from the first floor, the penthouse level more than made up for that.

She heard London speak in muffled tones, and heard his voice drop.

". . . Thanks for letting me know . . ."

When he reappeared without the food, Abigail knew better than to ask where it was. Instead, she waited until he was ready to explain.

"That wasn't the food," he said, "obviously. It was one of the attendants, a guy who's been pretty helpful since I got here. Gives me news briefs, updates on my hotels and staff, updates on my folks and sisters. Updates on English World, too."

She knew then what this was about.

"I don't know how to tell you this, Abigail. I know it's going to stress you out, but you have a right to know, and you'll find out sooner or later anyway."

"Is it about the missing administrative heads?"

"You knew?"

"Yeah, saw it on the way here. Amy Hart runs the Kyoto schools and Rick—Richard—Mulrooney is from Tokyo. But don't worry . . . they mentioned on the news that Amy had luggage missing. And my friend got a letter from English World saying to keep her safe they'd send her away for a little while, but to keep it quiet—"

"Which friend?" he interrupted.

"Savannah. So that's probably what happened with those two also. Or those three. I keep thinking it was only two since those were the pictures I saw."

"There *were* three, though."

"Yeah, did your guy say who the third one was?"

London pulled her to a standing position.

"He did. And Abigail, as nice as your theory is, I think you have to watch your back. Maybe even go home for a while."

"What are you talking about? Who was the third person?"

"The administrative head from Osaka."

"Osaka?" Abigail choked on the word.

"Yes. I think it's your friend. Savannah Thompson."

CHAPTER 10

Abigail signed the last of the congratulations cards she was sending out to her students. In the past, she'd put much more thought into them, much more enthusiasm. But this year . . . well . . . it was all she could do to etch out a congrats and thanks. She'd considered forgoing them altogether, but exam results had just come in, and despite the current situation with English World, the scores had improved by eight per cent this year. The students deserved some kind of acknowledgement for that.

She stretched as she walked over to the window. She stared at a tired ghost of herself in the window and rubbed her puffy eyes.

"At least the test scores will be good news for the teachers left at the meeting on Monday," she said to herself.

This morning, she'd received a fax from the utilities company. English World had failed to pay for electricity and now they would shut it off for four out of the five schools in Nagoya; the fifth would keep on using the deposit money. That bought just a little more time. She'd spent the day with Saori trying to reschedule lessons at the main school, the one that would still have lights and air conditioning, and then writing cards, when all she wanted to do was curl up at home and shut out the world.

I'm not ready to shut the schools down, she thought, *but I don't know how long I can keep this up. And I'm kind of starting not to care anymore.*

Abigail walked over to her locker. Savannah had been at the back of her thoughts all day. Of course. She wished she could call her now to talk through everything; everything always seemed a little clearer after talking things through with her. No, she wished she could call her now just to be sure she was okay.

She couldn't believe that Savannah would take the offer and leave without telling her, but she wasn't ready to believe the alternative: that someone had got to her before she'd been able to take the offer. This alternative would mean both her friend and her own sense of security would be gone.

She shivered at the thought and picked up the phone to call London. Spending the night in his secure hotel, in his secure arms, was what she needed tonight. Was it too late to call?

She looked at the little clock in the corner. Then at her phone. And back at the clock.

"No way!" she exclaimed in disbelief as she grabbed up everything she could and rushed out of the school, locking the door haphazardly as she left.

It was past midnight and the last train was leaving in minutes. Her savings were dwindling and she certainly didn't want to drop three thousand yen on a cab. She made it into the train just as the doors were closing and sank into the last seat open, next to a passed out Japanese businessman with *sake* emanating from his pores.

Abigail sighed, relaxing into her seat, letting the adrenaline drain away. She brought out a book from her bag and stared into it in an attempt to avoid eye contact with the subway of drunken men, who eyed her more obviously than on a daytime train.

Under usual circumstances she tried to avoid the last train. Five years of living in Japan had taught her that any politeness she was treated with during the day was thrown out on the last train home. She'd been groped, pushed, yelled at, cat-called, and propositioned.

Even now, she could feel a burning stare penetrating her skin, but she kept her head down. In her peripheral vision, she could see that there was an older Japanese man in a suit standing and holding onto a rail despite the empty seats around him. He swayed with the train, his eyes intent on her. The stare gave her chills, but she knew that if she lifted her eyes to meet his, it would only provoke whatever made him stare in the first place. Was it curiosity? Lust? Anger? Vengeance?

Vengeance. She shivered at the thought. She remembered feeling a little safer talking to Savannah when they came to the conclusion that the kidnapper was in Osaka, but now that her mind had time to wander, she remembered her twenty-five-minute train ride during her last visit to Savannah's neck of the woods. If someone was bent on abducting English World officials, Abigail was a quick train ride away from being the next victim.

She rummaged through her purse for her phone. London was one stop before hers, and she would just ask him to meet her at the station and let her sleep at his place.

"Dammit!" she cursed aloud. In the rush to leave English World, she had left her phone on the desk.

Abigail hoped the person at the front desk of The C Hotel would recognize her and let her in to call London because there was no way she was going to traverse the dark alleyways to get to her empty apartment. Not tonight.

At Kanayama station, the train nearly emptied. Abigail put her book away and looked up and everyone in sight was passed out. She craned her neck to look at the adjacent cars. No one staring from the distance, either. He was gone.

Maybe closing the schools would be a relief. Without sleep, and worrying that she could be in danger, she was unraveling. She would do some research tomorrow morning on other schools in the area and perhaps she could convince a school to accept some students from English World.

"Hibino. Hibino."

The announcement of London's station broke her from her plans and she scrambled off the train. Only a few people stumbled out of the train around her.

As Abigail emerged from the station into the warm, humid night air, she examined her surroundings. The other passengers had gone ahead of her while she had lingered in the safety of the train station, and now she was alone in the dark night.

The lights of Hibino were out for the night with the exception of London's hotel. She fixated it in her sights, took one more look around, and headed toward it with determination.

"OY!"

She heard the unbridled shout from behind her as she entered the darkest leg of her walk. A shiver ran down her spine. *It's just another drunk man wondering what a* gaijin *is doing in his neighborhood,* she told herself, but she quickened her pace, nonetheless.

"OY! *OMAE!*"

Any other time she would have turned around at such disrespectful language and given the speaker a piece of her mind, but this time the tone in the voice brought her terror and her walk turned into a jog. Her eyes focused on the illuminated *C* ahead of her, towering over the skyline.

She heard quickening footsteps behind her and, in moments, she felt two hands grasp her shoulders, spin her roughly, throw her back. She couldn't catch her balance and she tumbled backward into the side wall of a closed store.

She closed her eyes and blocked her face with her arms, expecting a blow. She could feel the adrenaline pulsing through her veins as her senses heightened. The concrete against her back pulled at her blouse, tearing it, scraping her skin. The even rougher hands of her attacker wrapped around her arms, fingernails digging into her skin, trying to pull her arms away from her face. The smell of cigarette smoke and booze filled her nostrils and caused her stomach to churn. She heard his strained, raspy breath for a moment before he spoke.

"How dare you . . ." the voice seethed in front of her.

The heavy accented English caught Abigail's attention and she opened her eyes tentatively. First she saw the wrinkled business suit.

"It's robbery!" he continued, shaking Abigail as he shouted. "They got what they deserved!"

A disgruntled student! She strained in the darkness to make out the face, lowering her arms for a clear view.

A full head of wild dark hair, graying at the roots. A scowling face, full of wrinkles. Bloodshot eyes. She recognized him in an instant.

"Atsushi! What are you doing?" she cried as she struggled to get away.

He brought his face close to hers. He was stronger than she would have ever thought in class.

"What am I doing?" he asked in a whisper. "What are *you* doing? What is English World doing? My son failed his English exam because of you and that damn school of yours!" He slammed her back into the wall again and threw her down to the ground.

She could feel her skin tearing as she slid against the ground, paralyzed in disbelief. Her mind flew through files of students in a desperate search for Atsushi's son until it reached the image of a 14-year-old Japanese boy with a round face, with hair that stood out from his scalp like grass and with premature bags under his eyes.

Atsushi always scheduled his son, Kenji, for private, one-on-one lessons, and whatever teacher was assigned to him winced at reading his name. He had a two-hour English lesson every day after two hours of math lessons and before two hours of classic Japanese. Kenji got home at 11:00 every night, run ragged by his father's expectations.

In the last lesson Abigail had had with him, Kenji had spent the entire lesson with his head in his hands, tugging at his hair. She'd tried so desperately to help him enjoy the lesson.

What is your favorite band?
I don't like music.
Do you like video games?
No.
Do you like anything?
No.
How was school?
Bad.
What do you like?
Nothing.

At the end of the lesson, Kenji was asleep in a layer of wispy hair on the desk. Her mind had spun with frustration and her heart had broken for the boy. She had often pleaded with his mother to lighten his load, but she'd always shaken her head, saying her husband wouldn't have it.

Abigail was brought back to her dangerous situation with a newfound fire in her blood. Atsushi was kneeling over her, a knee on her abdomen holding her down. His fists clenched, he cursed at her in Japanese. She boiled over, now with fight in her blood. Reaching up, she grabbed his suit jacket and yanked him to the side, freeing herself and throwing him off his balance.

If he'd been sober, he'd have been able to keep her there. But he wasn't.

She bolted to a crouching position and used the strength in her legs to pounce on him, bringing a fist squarely against his jaw. He tumbled down and she bounced up, kicking him in the ribs once, twice, before recognizing that Atsushi was now in the fetal position, begging her between gasps to stop.

She forced herself to step back. *I could kill him. I could strangle him right now while he's in pain and drunk beyond reason.*

She looked down on her student and knew she couldn't lower herself to beating someone once he was no longer a threat. She'd gained control of him. She could take back control of her own impulses. She threw the rest of her adrenaline into her words.

"You drunken bastard! How dare *you*? My teachers have been working without pay for creeps like you, who treat their children like objects. Your son is like an old man because of you! *That's* why he couldn't pass his test. Because you've destroyed him! *You're* the enemy."

Abigail's rant, not to mention the beating she'd given him, quieted Atsushi and he strained to comprehend her words. He struggled up and staggered toward her. She clenched her fist, ready and willing to take down this drunken bastard if he challenged her. Anger had replaced her fear, and now that she knew she was the stronger one in her sobriety and fury, she no longer felt the urge to run.

"My . . . son . . ." he muttered at her and stepped back, clawing his face.

He fell back against the wall into which he'd thrown Abigail only moments earlier and slumped down, his head falling into his hands.

She stared, relief and exhaustion replacing fear and fury. Then exhaustion took the forefront and her knees felt weak. Sweat and tears drenched her face—she'd been crying and she hadn't even realized it. Her back was wet from sweat and blood. Her knuckles were bloody, but it wasn't her own blood. She staggered toward The C Hotel, half-conscious of what she was doing, leaving Atsushi sobbing and broken against the wall.

❧

Abigail only became aware of her out-of-place appearance when she arrived in the pristine lobby. Every hard white angle contrasted with her torn clothing and body. Her legs could hardly hold her upright, but to rest on the white leather couches would keep her from London even longer.

"Miss, are you okay? Should I call a doctor?" a voice from behind asked.

It was the doorman to whom she'd spoken during her last visit. He remembered her.

"London . . . Crane . . . ," she forced out. "I need to see London Crane."

A spotless woman from the concierge desk approached, giving the doorman a sharp look for opening the hotel for this intruder, and for speaking to her. The woman eyed Abigail suspiciously, but picked up the phone.

"Mr. Crane? I'm sorry to bother you, but there's a . . . young lady . . . here to see you. Um . . . ," she turned her attention to Abigail, "what's your name?"

"Abigail Dennis."

She turned back to the call. "Mr. Crane? Hello?"

Moments later, London appeared in front of her and all her emotions overcame her. She wrapped her arms around his neck.

Without a word, London's arms enveloped her and held her tight. He also took note of the torn clothing and bloodied hands. He led her to the elevator and held her in silence until they arrived in his suite. He sat her down on his bed and kissed her forehead, smoothing her hair.

"I . . . I . . . ," she started. "Atsushi . . . a student . . . he followed me and attacked me."

London gathered her up in one arm and dialed a number with the other hand.

"Yes . . . English? Do you speak English? *Eigo?* Oh! Oh, thank you! My name is London Crane. There's been an attack on my girlfriend. I need a police officer and a doctor. Can you send them to The C hotel at Hibino, Penthouse 2? Thank you, thank you!"

He touched a fingertip to her chin and tilted her head so their eyes met. "Are you okay for a moment if I get a washcloth?"

When she nodded, he rushed to the bathroom and emerged with a cool, wet washcloth and sat beside Abigail. With one arm around her, he gently wiped her face and hands, and just as gently prodded for more information.

She was exhausted and, in the comfort of London's arms, she had to fight to stay awake and recount her experience to London, knowing that she'd need to recount it again just minutes later to the police, but his aqua eyes were full of fear and concern and she couldn't leave him that way.

"And the strange thing is, I felt so out of control. It was scary. When he attacked me, I was terrified, but when I came out of fighting back, I was so scared at how easily I could have killed him."

"You were fighting for your life."

"You don't know that. He pushed me, he grasped me and held me down. He yelled and looked like he would hit me, but how do I know if he would have killed me?"

"What are you saying? Whether he was going to kill you or not, you had every right to fight back. I'm proud of you for doing it."

"I've never felt so out of control," she sobbed.

"You defended yourself." London pounded a fist onto his thigh as he said half to himself, "I should have been there. You shouldn't have had to fight. You shouldn't have had to fear at all—"

A knock at the door stopped London's further protests and a cynical expression spread across his face. "At least I can do something. It pays to be a Crane."

Abigail smiled at his joke, but her heart ached for his guilt.

NIHON NIGHTS

She sighed. Her body ached. Her eyes watered. And she was so emotionally tired she couldn't focus on the questions from the officers. The doctor had cleaned and dressed her wounds and all she wanted to do was sleep until Monday.

"Did Atsushi-*san* ever take lessons in any other cities?"

"Um, I don't know. He traveled for work a lot. On Monday I can get his files from the English World office. Can we finish this then?"

The officer did not look up from his notebook and wrote furiously.

"And you said you knew Miss Savannah Thompson?"

She was getting frustrated. She could answer these questions just as well, if not better, on Monday.

"I *know* Savannah, yes. We're friends. Can we please finish this on Monday?"

"And did Mr. Atsushi know Miss Thompson?"

"I . . . don't . . . know. Not through me, but like I said before, the records at English World would let you know where he took his lessons. You also have Saori's information; she can help you navigate the computer system."

The officer either finally honored Abigail's request or figured he wasn't going to get any more quality information from interrogating her tonight. He bowed deeply and handed her his card before replacing his cap on his head.

"If you think of anything more, please call at any time. We have Atsushi-san in custody, so you should be safe. I will call Miss Saori for Atsushi's files."

He bowed once more and marched out the door.

London gently helped her undress and laid her down on his bed. The bed was softer and more comfortable than she remembered it from her last night there. In fact, she could barely remember the bed at all, only what happened in it. She smiled at the memory, wishing she could muster up the strength for some physical activity to take her mind off the outside world, but the bed beckoned her. She felt the warmth of London's body next to hers, a heavy arm on her waist and a gentle kiss before she surrendered to sleep.

❦

The morning light streamed through the sheer curtain of the pristine room, and after a moment of scowling at the light for waking her, Abigail appreciated how warm London's "cold" suite felt. She sat up and looked around the room, rubbing her sore muscles. London was not in sight, nor was there any evidence he was anywhere in the suite, but on the table near the balcony, a glass of orange juice caught her attention.

She slid out of the bed and slipped London's discarded button-up shirt over her bare shoulders. She focused on the orange juice, wanting to fight off thoughts of last night's struggle as long as she could.

The delicate glass table, near the open door to the balcony, had a square glass vase filled with fresh calla lilies. Abigail sat in the white leather chair and scanned the traditional American breakfast spread out in front of her. It was a far cry from the rice ball she grabbed on the way to work so many mornings. The colors stood out vividly against the white backdrop of the suite. Her eyes stopped when they reached a piece of paper with *The C* written with gold embossing at the top.

Dearest Abigail,

I had to step out this morning and did not want to wake you. I have a security guard watching the entrance to the suite to ensure your safety. Please relax and recover. I'll be back shortly.

Love,
London

She returned her focus to the table and grabbed for the bacon with one hand and the orange juice with the other as she looked through the open door. It was amazing that she could feel so calm and happy here in London's room, when everything around her was crumbling.

She felt so disconnected from her world here, but she had to return to it to help her students and her teachers. She spotted London's Macbook and brought it to the breakfast table with her and accessed her email.

There was still no word from Savannah. Even if she had left Japan in a hurry without telling her, Abigail had hoped Savannah would have at least emailed her to let her know she was safe at home. She opened up a new email and started adding the names of all of the teachers and staff left in Japan. She looked through the open door again. Last night she had been able to take care of herself, and now it was her responsibility to take care of her teachers.

My dedicated teachers and staff,

You have no doubt heard of the new missing administrative heads, and some of you may even know them personally. I do. I have spoken with authorities and they are working as hard as they can to find them. If you have any information at all that you think would be useful to them, let me know so that we can help in any way possible.

In addition to this, I have a little more bad news. On Friday, I received statements from the utilities companies. English World has not paid for utilities here in Nagoya, and, on Monday, four of our five schools will no longer have electricity or water and must obviously be closed.

I had planned to give you this news on Monday at our weekly meeting, but I'm afraid that I will need to cancel that as well for security purposes. Last night, a very irate student followed me from the school. I'm fine and have notified the police, but I'm afraid for the time being we must cancel classes.

I still would like to meet with you at the Starbucks at Kanayama Station at ten o'clock Monday morning to check in and decide together the next step for our students and ourselves. Also, I would appreciate it if everyone who receives this email responds so that I may know that you are all safe. I suggest you avoid traveling alone.

I appreciate all of your support and dedication during this difficult time and I hope not to cause any unwarranted fear or worry. We will figure something out.

With gratitude,
Abigail Dennis

As soon as she sent the email, she felt invigorated. Her world was crumbling, but she was not hiding from it. She was facing it and working together with her colleagues to find a solution and keep everyone safe.

The doorknob twisted and London appeared in his *Slow Hand Jam* t-shirt, board shorts and flip-flops. She rushed to greet him and he gathered her up in his arms, pressing his lips to hers.

"The breakfast was very nice, London, thank you. As much as I like Japanese food, it sure is comforting having a little taste of home."

London stepped back and examined her. "Looks like you're feeling much better."

"Much. I hope you don't mind that I used your laptop. I left my phone at the school last night, and I usually use that to check email when I'm away from home."

"Not at all."

"I emailed the remaining teachers and staff. We're going to meet on Monday at Starbucks to plan the next move for our students."

London's smile faded and concern took over. He guided her back to the table and sat down next to her, setting an envelope on the table.

"Abigail, do you really think it's safe for you to stay? I'm sure there are other students who failed their exams . . . and admin heads are starting to go missing. Including your friend. And then you were attacked last night. Whether or not Atsushi is connected to the missing people, it is a sign that things are not altogether safe for you here right now."

"Well, I'm not going to run away. The police officer said I would be safe, and they're keeping tabs on me. I defended myself last night."

"And look at you! You're all cut up! What if he hadn't been drunk? What if he'd had a knife?"

She placed her hand on his arm. "London, I'm fine. Really."

He handed her the envelope.

"Two open-ended return flights to San Diego. I think you should go home for a while. I'd love to visit San Diego, too, if you'll have me along. The tickets are first-class."

She pushed his hand and the envelopes back to the table. "I *am* home. I'm not leaving."

"Just for a little while . . ."

"And leave my teachers and students stranded here while I take a *vacation*?"

"It's not safe for you here!"

She let out a frustrated sigh and slipped into her slacks from last night, grabbed her purse and looked back at him. How many times did she have to reiterate this to him?

"I took care of myself for five years here before you arrived. Nagoya is home to me."

She looked at him once more before she walked out the door and made her way out of The C.

He didn't follow.

CHAPTER 11

Abigail knew she shouldn't have stormed out so damn dramatically, and inside her the argument continued.

He was only trying to be helpful. But he should have asked before buying the tickets. Just buying them implied that she would drop her responsibilities to go wherever he told her to.

He was concerned for her safety. She had come to the hotel in quite a mess the night before. But he should have asked what would be helpful to her, not just assumed he knew best. And he shouldn't have insisted she do anything; that was up to her to decide.

Abigail shook her head and glanced across the street. She hadn't been paying attention as she walked, and here she was standing across from the attack site from the night before. She fought the urge to walk on, ignore it, bury it. Instead, she squared her shoulders and mustered up the courage to cross the road.

"Oh my . . . ," she muttered when she noticed the droplets of blood staining the cement. Was it her blood or Atsushi's? A chill ran over her, and she felt exposed.

She'd never been so scared in her life, but it hadn't crossed her mind that those moments might be her last. The adrenaline had kicked in and she'd simply fought.

Now she wondered if Atsushi would have killed her. Maybe he was just taking out his frustration, maybe he was so used to taking out his aggression on his son and wife when he didn't get his way that he felt he could do so with Abigail as well. Though the police seemed to imply that he was responsible for the English World kidnappings, she felt it didn't seem the way he would carry out his rage. And besides, she'd been able to fight him off, so why couldn't Richard Mulrooney, who had done some small-time boxing back home in Britain?

Of course, hadn't she decided that the "missing" people were just folks who'd taken English World's offer and moved away for a while? Hadn't Amy Hart packed luggage? Hadn't Savannah gotten an offer to go away?

But what about Richard? And the corporate folks? And why didn't Savannah at least call her back?

Abigail moved past the site, determined not to let her fear from the night before pour in and cloud the present situation. At the train station, she bought a can of coffee from the "hot drinks" vending machine and waited, ready to be home and at the same time wishing she were back in London's hotel, in his arms.

❦

The four-apartment complex looked quaint after a night in The C, but she was glad to see it. She'd lived here four of the five years she had been in Nagoya, and that history comforted her now.

She opened the front door into the tiny foyer. A pile of shoes, many more than the number of residents, sat in the corner of the wooden floor. She removed her own with deft movements, so good at it by now that she didn't need to touch her shoes with her hands, nor bend down. The toe of one shoe loosened the other heel, then vice versa, and with two kicks they were off.

She slid them to the pile in the corner and then turned to the four doors in front of her. Abigail knew only one of her neighbors, she realized now. Catering to foreigners, the turn-over was so great that getting to know someone seemed to foreshadow their departure. But the Frenchman who shared a wall with her had been here a while and she knew him simply because he often left his apartment door open. He smiled at her now.

"*Bonjour.*" She saluted with a wave.

He set down the book he'd been reading and lifted himself off the low sofa on which he was lounging. Did he always leave his door open because he wanted to chat? Was he lonely?

Abigail was not feeling lonely and really preferred just to get inside her own place and relax. Recuperate.

"*Ah, bonjour,* Abigail," he cooed as he reached his open front door. His tongue sounded thick against the syllables of her name. She didn't particularly find his skinny frame and shag haircut appealing, but no one could argue they didn't like to hear their name in that accent.

"I'm just going to my apartment. I'll catch up with you another time," she explained, pressing her key into the door, trying to politely excuse herself.

"You did not come in last night. I think," he winked at her, "you must finally be in love."

Abigail stared at him. What business was it of his? And when did he start keeping track of her comings and goings? Just because he left his door open most of the time, was he now the building warden?

"I had a rough night," she offered. "I'm going to rest now."

He leaned against his doorframe. "*Oui, a bien tot.*"

"See you later."

With a turn of the knob and a step and a closing of the door, she was finally alone.

But what was on the floor? Abigail bent down to scoop up the paper under her feet. It wasn't time for the utility bills just yet, and all other mail would go to the little mailboxes at the front of the building.

She straightened her back, examined the blank envelope. Could be apartment communication. They used the mail slot in the door as well, but what would they want? She was up to date on her rent . . . though for how long she wasn't sure.

Abigail opened the window and flipped on the fan before sinking into the chair at her kitchen table and tearing open the envelope.

The familiar English World stationary caught her eye, simply because it had been a while since they'd sent anything other than email. Maybe it was all over after all.

But this was addressed to her directly, and bold red letters across the top warned:

CONFIDENTIAL.

She dropped the sheet of paper on the table and leaned back in her chair a moment. She contemplated making a cup of tea, taking a shower, taking a nap, before reading the letter. Nothing "confidential" that English World had to say at this point was going to be good news.

"Well, hell," she muttered, picked up the letter again and hunkered down for the bad news.

Dear Ms. Abigail Dennis:

As you know, Mr. Inudori has been missing for several weeks. Additional executives have disappeared, as have three administrative heads. We have some information not available to the media that points to foul play, and are writing you since you may be a possible target for additional kidnappings.

English World does not have the resources to relocate all staff, but we have set aside limited funds to protect some key managers who are most at risk. You are one of these, and we offer you a trip out of Japan until the danger subsides, at which time we will facilitate your return.

PLEASE KEEP THIS LETTER AND OFFER CONFIDENTIAL. We cannot afford to relocate all staff, and making this offer may raise questions of funds and require us to remove the offer altogether.

We encourage you to consider this offer. If you are interested, please call us at the below secured phone number and we will arrange a flight. If you are not interested, please destroy this letter, and please do take measures on your own to keep safe.

Abigail set the letter on the table gingerly and smoothed it with her palm.

"I'm important enough to get my own offer," she announced. "Then again, I'm important enough to be a target, whatever that means."

Abigail thought back to Richard Mulrooney, Amy Hart, and, of course, Savannah. They must have all received offer letters. Savannah was going to take hers, but then she just disappeared. Amy obviously took hers, having packed as she did. Richard . . . who knew?

"Where are you, Savannah?"

Abigail moved to her bedroom and pulled her laptop onto her lap while sinking into the futon. She didn't have Savannah's parents' contact information, but she had her sister's email address, gathered during the sister's visit to Japan one summer. Abigail had played tour guide for Nagoya on a weekend when Savannah had prior plans.

She typed a quick message—she didn't want to worry anyone. A question, just one.

Did Savannah come home this week?

The reply was almost instant, in the kind of modern shorthand that meant she'd sent it from her smartphone.

Said she would. But ticket was for somewhere else. HW—lucky. Didn't say bye?

Abigail wrote back, *H. W.? No, she was going to come by this weekend, but then she just . . .* She struggled for the right word. Vanished? That was what had happened . . . *left. Any word from her?*

Again, the reply was quick.

HW=Hawaii. Set her up in resort. Txt me when she arrived, said it was humid but no more than Osaka.

Abigail breathed a sigh of relief. *So she's okay then?*

OK? Why wouldn't she be?

There was no way Abigail would give her all the scary details. *Just asking. Glad she arrived safely. Why are you up so late?*

With a boy. GG.

"Gotta go. I'll bet," Abigail translated aloud with a laugh, her spirits lightening.

Savannah was in Hawaii. And she wondered if she accepted the English World offer if she'd be sent there, too. Maybe she and Savannah's time together would be spent gallivanting at the beach or eating fresh pineapple.

It was actually rather tempting, she realized. She wasn't entirely convinced that she was in any real danger, but a vacation in Hawaii . . . ? A *paid* vacation in Hawaii? With one of her favorite friends? Tempting, indeed.

Then again, if she was fine with taking their offer, hopping a little plane to some Hawaiian resort to lay low a while and hang out with Savannah, why had she fought so vehemently with London about his offer? Was she that intent on proving to him that she was independent?

London. What would he think if she were to go missing suddenly? The letter said to tell no one, for her own safety. Maybe if she packed luggage, too. Left a letter, but didn't say where she was going? Then again, hadn't London emphasized the "trust that surrounded" her?

Trust and truth went hand-in-hand.

No, she wouldn't take the offer. She'd stick around, stick it out. London was willing to place security wherever she wanted it, and that was more than the other folks had had. And it had to be enough to keep her safe, though admittedly she'd have to make amends with London first and foremost.

❧

Abigail decided to stop by the school office before the ten o'clock meeting at Starbucks. She wanted to put up a sign for parents, students, and any staff that might have missed her email that the school was temporarily closed.

The main office was one of the few buildings not to have power shut off yet but Abigail had not expected to find the lights on inside. She unlocked the glass door quickly, then paused. Maybe she ought not to go inside. Suppose someone was in there that shouldn't be.

She looked around. A few people passed on the street, but the main Monday morning rush hadn't yet begun. Abigail turned the lock and stepped away from the door and searched in her bag for her cell phone.

"Darn it," she muttered, remembering she'd left it inside the night before. She stood in front of the school, trying to decide whether it was safe to go in.

Suddenly a face appeared on the other side of the glass door. Abigail's heart leapt into her throat and she jumped back.

It took a couple seconds before she recognized the face. "Saori!"

Saori opened the door, registering Abigail's alarmed expression.

"Abigail! Were you trying to get in? I heard the lock turn, and thought I heard your voice outside."

Abigail caught her breath before answering. "Yes. Oh, my goodness, I'm so glad it was you in there."

Saori looked more tired than ever as she held the door wide for Abigail to enter.

"I was not expecting you," Saori admitted, moving back to the reception desk and an open schedule, marked with scratches and white-out applied and reapplied. "I thought we were meeting at Starbucks at ten."

"We are. So why are you here?"

Saori looked sheepishly at Abigail and then back at her schedule book. "Still trying to catch up. There are not enough teachers for all the students, Abigail."

"I know that."

"And now, with some schools closing, we don't have enough room to consolidate. I have been trying to work it out."

Saori held up the schedule book, and Abigail saw arrows and cross-outs and lists of options with Xs through them. It could have been a football playbook. She went to Saori's side and took the book from her, closed it, and tucked it under an arm.

"You can't solve this with logistics, Saori," she said, touching her forearm. "And you can't solve this alone. Come to Starbucks at ten and we'll all brainstorm together on what options we have. Until then, feel free to rest in the back. Shall I make you some tea?"

"No . . . actually, yes. That would be nice."

Abigail stopped in her office to pick up her phone, and then moved toward the kitchen and called back to Saori, "Not sure we have a lot left, but if we have any ramen, do you want me to make you some? I need to go to the market again."

But Saori was behind her.

"Oh!" Abigail exclaimed, "You startled me! I thought you were still up front."

"You said I should come back here and rest."

"I guess I did."

"I wanted to say, you do not need to go to the market. The new teacher, London Crane, has brought food for the kitchen."

Abigail looked at Saori briefly, then quickened her pace to the kitchen.

Sure enough, the cupboards were full of noodles and rice and the small fridge even held some fresh veggies and milk.

"London brought these?"

"Yes. He said he wanted to give you a break from shopping this week. He is a very nice man."

Abigail took in the vibrant colors of the vegetables before closing the fridge door. "Yes, he is," she answered absently.

❦

The meeting at Starbucks included fewer people than Abigail had anticipated. The several attendees seemed mainly interested in whether they could still get food from the school kitchen, and Abigail gave full credit to London for restocking. Once the teachers heard of the delicacies London had provided, they were distracted, obviously anxious to get first dibs on the food.

London hadn't even shown, and Abigail wondered if she'd burned her bridges with the first man who'd kept her attention since moving to Japan. She still wasn't happy that he felt he knew what was best for her, but she couldn't help feeling sorry not to see him there.

When Abigail noticed the frappuccinos, iced mochas, and iced teas were nearly drained, she knew she couldn't hold the group much longer.

"Okay, then," she announced, looking over her notes. "We came up with a few things I think we can implement immediately.

"First, the lecture format. I'll send out an email this afternoon to say all regular classes have been canceled, but that those interested may attend a daily lecture we'll be offering. Seats will be on a first-come, first-served basis, and everyone else can stand. They'll run two hours, with a ten-minute break in the middle, and focus primarily on English grammar and vocab."

"How do we know who should do the lectures?" a teacher asked.

Another spoke up, answering before Abigail could even think up a response. She sure did like this open and communal format.

"Why don't we each take one day? There are only five of us here."

"And Abigail and Saori, but they can coordinate."

"Did that new teacher go home already?"

Abigail's ears perked up, but she didn't reply.

"I don't think so. I'm surprised he isn't here, though."

Saori looked at Abigail, sharing their secret. Of course, she didn't know the half of it. Abigail spoke up.

"Let's leave London Crane out of the rotation, but we'll have him fill in if needed. I like the idea of one person a day, but let's have the teacher for the following day attend the prior day's lecture as well. That way they can help if things get out of hand, and they'll know what was just covered, and what kinds of questions came up. So everyone will be working for two hours—maybe three with prep—twice a week. That will give you time to do some job hunting if you need to."

"Um . . . do we need to?" one teacher asked hesitantly.

How should she reply? Truthfully? If she did, even her last five teachers would be gone soon. Then again, how long until all the power was off and they'd be gone anyhow.

"I think so," she replied quietly. "I don't know how long it is going to take English World to dig themselves out of this mess. If they do, and they still have me as administrative head, I'll hire you back if you want to come back, regardless if you leave now or not."

After the mildly fruitful meeting, Saori approached her.

"We didn't solve everything," she noted, stating the obvious.

"I'm afraid not. But we have a work-around."

"Shall I go back to the schedule book?"

"No . . . let's just go with the lecture idea. It won't be as productive, but at least exams are over, so it may not have as much of an impact. Can you email the teachers the rotation, one day per person as teacher, with the following teacher observing?"

"Yes, I will."

"And I'll email the students. Oh, and Saori, let's keep the school door locked from now on. You don't need to deal with angry parents and students, and nothing they say will help the situation."

As Saori walked away, Abigail noticed her shoulders slouched. Perhaps she was finally feeling defeated, too.

CHAPTER 12

London was waiting on her apartment doorstep when she arrived home.

"How long have you been waiting? It's a furnace out here!"

He wasn't sweating at all, and Abigail followed his line of sight to a white car with dark windows parked across the street. The driver nodded, then pulled out, driving away without a word.

"Don't make me sound so heroic." He laughed. "Yaz has cars just for her hotel; she let me use one. It's got air conditioning. When I saw you coming, I got out and waited here. Didn't want you to worry, you know, with a car watching your apartment and all."

"I see. Maybe we should have talked in the car then, if it's cool." She laughed and felt her body loosen up.

He was here. He hadn't left. He raised an eyebrow, but stayed quiet.

She pushed open the door. "Come on in."

"I know you're going to offer to make tea, because you always do," London said as they entered the apartment and then the kitchen. She motioned him toward the table and chairs. "But it's too damn hot for tea, Abigail."

She laughed. "Lukewarm tap water then?"

TRISHA HADDAD and MONICA HADDAD

He approached her, drew something from the messenger bag strapped across his wide chest, and held it to her neck before she could see what it was.

She shrieked.

"Aaack! That's COLD!"

He withdrew the can of Pepsi and popped the top. "Ice cold Pepsi, just for you."

"That was surprising, but good heavens, refreshing, too! Hand it over!"

"I brought something else, too. I'm sure it isn't as good as the ones at home, but what can you do?"

He lifted a pineapple from his bag, and Abigail's mouth watered. It had been so long since she'd had fresh pineapple; even the canned stuff was a little out of her price range here for regular consumption.

"Ooo, that looks good. Let me get a knife."

"I can cut it," he offered, taking the blade from her hand and leading her to the kitchen table. "You gotta do it the right way. And besides, it's my present for you. I'll do it fast, though, so it stays cold. You enjoy that soda."

She sat down and took a sip. It was crisp and ice cold and the little bubbles played on her tongue.

"How did you keep everything so cold? How high was the air conditioning in that car?"

He laughed and sliced.

"There's a cooler in the car. I think they usually use it for champagne and stuff like that. But it was perfect for my surprise, too."

Abigail took another sip and sighed, clasping her hands around the can—narrower than the ones in the

185

U.S.—and looking down at the table. Her eyes fell on the English World letter and she surreptitiously folded it and pushed it into her pocket. If he saw it, London would open up the discussion again about her leaving. Abigail didn't think he'd tell her to take the English World offer—it would infuriate him that they weren't paying staff but were paying for people to leave. No, it would just bring up his own offer again, and she'd be left explaining the plan the group had come up with for the school and how she wanted to see it through for the teachers who had stuck around, and how, for goodness sakes, she didn't want to feel pressured or controlled.

No, he couldn't see the letter.

Then he was right beside her, a finger on her chin, tilting her head up.

"Take this pineapple into your mouth, but don't chew it yet."

He placed a small square on her tongue, and she closed her mouth. It was harder than she had expected not to chew it and swallow. He lowered himself into the chair next to her.

"Close your eyes. Good, isn't it? Can you feel the juices start to seep out, without you even chewing? Seep onto your tongue and slip down your throat?"

Abigail couldn't answer with her mouth full of pineapple, but she nodded with eyes still closed. She felt heat rise in her neck and cheeks.

"Hold the flesh against the roof of your mouth with your tongue, and swallow the juices down. Now the flesh is rougher, grainier, but even more inviting, isn't it? Okay, chew—no, not fast. Just a movement or two at a time, feel how the flesh breaks apart against your teeth. Swallow the juice down with each movement. And when you can't hold on any longer—yes, now. Swallow what is left of the pineapple."

Abigail's eyes fluttered open and she swallowed. London was looking at her expectantly.

"Never enjoyed pineapple so much, huh?"

"No . . . ," she breathed.

"This is not your canned chunk pineapple. And just wait until you visit Maui with me someday. Then you'll really taste pineapple."

Abigail stood, stepped toward his chair and threw a leg over, settling on his lap. "There you go," she cooed, playing, flirting, "telling me what to do again."

His hands found her waist and traced down to her hips before pulling her closer.

"How could I forget? You prefer to be the boss."

She leaned down and her lips met his, smiling. "I *am* the boss. Preference has nothing to do with it."

"And what do you want from me, then?"

"For you to stop telling me what to do."

"Well, that's boring, Abigail. I was hoping you'd want something else."

"Maybe I do." She leaned down for another kiss, her tongue lingering on the fleshy inside of his lower lip. "But first I want you to promise to let me make my own choices."

"You're making it hard for me not to promise. This is sort of blackmail, you know."

Abigail felt between her legs and through his jeans a hardening, and London shifted uncomfortably. Straddling him, she rode right along with his squirming.

"Promise." She stood up, still over him.

"Fine," he declared, pulling her back down onto his lap, "I promise! I'll let you decide what you want to do. So long as you let me be part of it. And so long as, for goodness sakes, you stop making such a big deal out of it."

Abigail reached over to the plate of squared pineapple chunks London had set on the table. Picking up one juicy piece with her fingers, she placed it between her teeth and leaned forward. London's lips brushed hers as he took the piece, sucked the juice, dissolved the flesh.

She pulled at his t-shirt, guided it over his head and watched as the blond curls fell back around his aqua eyes. She grabbed another hunk of pineapple, placed it between her teeth and then leaned down to trail it over his throat and across his collar bones, before chewing and swallowing the fruit.

"That juice is sticky—" he began.

But she leaned back down and rested her tongue against the sharp edge of his collar bone, flicked it across, tasting the sweet yet tart pineapple juice. At his throat, she lapped it up, and then planted her mouth against his.

"We good then?" she whispered.

"Hell yeah," he replied.

And after that, there were no more words.

Abigail awoke to London pacing the floor in just a pair of red silk boxers, looking from his phone to the window and back at his phone. Dawn had nearly broken, and the misty mauve light played across his thick shoulder blades. The muscles in his neck tensed.

"London?" she muttered groggily.

He startled, turned toward her. "Did I wake you? I was trying to be quiet."

"What are you doing? Come back to bed."

She lifted the thin sheet up, inviting him in with her open arms framing her nude body. He glanced at her and she saw the boxers jump slightly, but he turned away.

"I can't. I . . . I just got a text from Yaz, Abigail. She thought I ought to know something . . . just came across the news wire. Thought *you* ought to know it, anyway."

Abigail sat up, wrapping the sheet around her body. "What is it?"

London's pacing started up again, only quicker this time. In her small room, and with his long legs, a few paces one way and he'd be turned back the other way.

"You know Richard Mulrooney, right?"

"Of course. Admin head that went missing the same day as Amy Hart." She paused and then added, "And Savannah."

"Damn, how do I say this? I didn't even know the fellow, and I'm gonna have a hard time saying it. I'll just do it, then . . ."

Abigail stood up, tucking the sheet around her body like a towel. She stopped him in his tracks.

"What is it, London? Just say it."

His aqua eyes pierced into hers.

"He's dead, Abigail. They've found his body. He was murdered."

∼⬧∽

She paced the room now, and he sat on the futon, his head in his hands. "I know I told you I wouldn't bring it up again."

"Don't, then," she warned him. "Please. I need to think."

He stood and caught her in her pacing. His fingers tenderly wrapped around her upper arms.

"Do you think you could be a target, too, Abigail?"

"I don't know."

But then her mind rushed back to the offer letter. English World thought she might be a target and was willing to spend some of its little remaining money getting her to safety.

Of course, Amy Hart and Savannah were safe. Amy had packed and Savannah had gotten an offer to go. Her sister confirmed she'd landed in Hawaii.

"Where was he found?"

London checked the text message again. "Yaz doesn't say. She just said it came through the wire and wanted me to be sure you were safe."

Abigail opened her laptop and waited for it to boot up. Then she searched for information.

"In Japan," she whispered, half to herself. "He was found here."

"In Nagoya?"

"No, in Tokyo. A few blocks from his apartment."

"Abigail," London said, testing the words, "would you be willing to let me assign you some security?"

He waited, as though sure she'd round on him.

She surprised him. "That's a good idea. I'm not against being safe, London. So yes, please do. That would be nice of you."

"Maybe at your apartment door? And the school? And I can send a car to drive you."

She closed the laptop with a dull thud, fury spreading through her at the situation. Richard Mulrooney was dead. Nice guy, highly efficient manager, good person. Prime of his life, cut short, and for what?

English World?

"I'm closing the school," she announced.

"What?"

"I'm closing that damn school. It isn't worth this. Rick's life. And who knows who else? English World isn't worth it. The students are great, but their exam scores aren't worth it."

"And the teachers?"

"The teachers deserve better than English World."

CHAPTER 13

The next day the school doors were locked, and the school was vacant. Abigail had called each teacher individually and offered her place if they got turned out of the English World apartments at any time, and told them she'd stock her kitchen with staples they were welcome to. All they had to do was call to say they were coming over.

And she wished them the best of luck in their job search, asking that they list her as a reference if they needed one.

When, at nearly midnight, Abigail heard a rapping on the door, she wondered not if it were a kidnapper or a murderer, or even if one of London's security guards had to use her bathroom, but if someone was taking her up on her offer.

She wrapped her light kimono robe around her and thought of London in his suite at The C. He'd asked her to stay with him, but after the long day tying up loose ends, and several teachers coming in the morning for food, she'd told him to plan on her around noon the next day. Now she wished she was there with him already, not twelve hours and twenty minutes from seeing him again.

Bending slightly, she looked through the peep hole, surprised by the visitor on the other side. Abigail threw the door open.

"Saori! What brings you here at this hour!"

Saori shifted from one foot to the other. Her short mini-skirt and platform shoes, paired with a modest turtleneck and huge hoop earrings, hinted that she'd been out that night. The glitter eye shadow was smeared enough that Abigail knew she was not just heading out now, but likely heading home.

Still she didn't answer, and didn't make eye contact, hugging her arms around her torso as though she were cold. It was anything but cold in Nagoya in the summer. Even at night. Even tonight.

"How rude of me," Abigail continued. "Please come in."

Saori slipped her shoes off silently and set them next to the door, away from the main pile of shoes in the apartment foyer.

Once inside Saori looked around, and Abigail realized she'd never had Saori over before. She must have had access to the address, of course; it had been in Abigail's recent email to teachers and staff.

"I was going to wait until tomorrow to hand out more food, but if you came all the way over here for that, I'd be happy to give you some now. You should know, the last trains leave my station at midnight, so I don't want to keep you—"

"I did not come for food. I will try to be quick in why I came, and get back to the train station."

"Have a seat," Abigail offered, pulling one out. She put on a pot of water and pulled out two tea bags from the cupboard without asking if Saori would have tea with her. The *kanji* for trust blazed red against the black kettle.

"Now, while that's heating up, tell me what's going on."

Saori was examining her fingernails, but then she looked up suddenly.

"I was out . . . well, obviously," she looked down at her clothes. "I was out with friends and one was reading the news streaming on her phone. It is more bad news, Abigail, and I wanted to come to tell you before you see it tomorrow on the newsstands or the Internet."

"Richard Mulrooney?"

"No, I saw your email. I know you know about Mr. Mulrooney." She dropped her chin and shook her head.

"Then what is it?"

The sudden shriek of the kettle made them both jump, and Abigail rushed to pull it off the stove.

"Don't want to wake the neighbors," she whispered, grabbing two tea cups and placing a bag in each. After pouring the hot water, she brought two spoons and saucers with her to the table.

"It's Chinese flower tea. Delicious. Now, please, continue."

Saori looked at her huge pink watch, one she'd never wear to work. "Only ten more minutes, and really, only five minutes before I have to leave to walk over. No, let me call my mother. She will come to pick me up."

"Will she be awake at this time?" Abigail asked, anxious to find out the rest of the news. Why didn't Saori just come out with it already?

"No, it will wake her. But it must be done. May I stay a while here, while she drives into town?"

"You know what? Don't worry about it. Just wait here a sec." Abigail walked into her room and reemerged with her cell phone. "London has his drivers on call, so someone must be up at this time. I'll have one of them drive you home. Safer than the train anyhow."

"London Crane?"

Abigail looked up, met Saori's eyes. "Um . . . yes."

She waited for the additional questions, but Japanese politeness won out. Abigail's position of authority in the job she no longer had really won out. Saori didn't ask for clarification, and after she realized clarification was not going to be freely offered, her curiosity melted back into her prior anxiety.

Abigail settled the matter with the driver on call, who would be there within ten minutes, and would wait outside the apartment as long as need be. Then she settled back into the chair, removing the tea bag from her cup.

"Okay," she sighed. "Now you have all the time in the world." *But please don't take that long*, she urged silently.

"Thank you. I was out with my friend . . ."

"Yes, and your friend was reading the news."

"No, looking at streaming news. Headlines."

"On her phone, yes. What did she see?"

"I didn't want you to just find out tomorrow in the train station on your way out."

Saori looked up at the wall, scanned the photographs there. Abigail followed her gaze to the photograph of Savannah bundled up against the glorious snow-chilled Sapporo during a week vacation two years back. Savannah was wearing Abigail's extra scarf, after having dropped hers in a puddle moments after leaving their hostel.

After seeing what Saori was focusing on, Abigail snapped her head back to her guest.

"Find out what?" she insisted, the fear rising within her.

"My friend was reading the headlines and asked the name of the administrative head at my branch. I told her Ms. Abigail Dennis, from the United States. She asked me, 'Your boss is not Ms. Savannah Thompson?' "

"I know she's missing."

"She has been found."

"Found where? In Hawaii?"

"Hawaii? No. Osaka. On a train." Saori's eyes began to mist. "I know she was your very close friend."

"She was on a train?" Abigail hardly knew what was happening. She decided that if Saori didn't come out with it about five seconds, she'd run to her laptop and look it up herself.

"They are trying to find information. Security videos show a man carrying her in. Motioned to another passenger to . . . shhh . . . be quiet. Like she was sleeping. Not many people on late trains. Videos in another station show him getting off the train. Can't see his face. She is not with him."

"He left her sleeping on the train?" Abigail thought of the creeps she'd come across on the last trains of the night. Panic rose against her throat. "Is she okay? Did someone hurt her?"

"When the train retired for the night, crews came through and found her."

"Is she okay?"

"No. She has passed away . . ." Saori's usually-fluent English deteriorated into sobs. "Murdered. Bullet in the back of the head. Hat covering. Dead."

The room spun. This couldn't be correct. Saori's friend had read it wrong. Or Saori was translating it wrong. Savannah was in Hawaii. She'd called her sister from the airport. She was there; she'd taken the flight.

No . . . she'd taken English World's offer. She was safe.

But she was going to go later. What if she *had* been kidnapped. That would explain why she never came to Nagoya, why she didn't tell Abigail she was in Hawaii. What if she didn't take the offer in time. Before they got her.

Who? Who got her? And what was *got*?

"No . . . ," she muttered.

Saori dropped her eyes to the table, unsure of how she should respond. How she could comfort her boss.

"No . . ." Abigail repeated. "She called her sister from Hawaii. She called and said she was in Hawaii. She took the offer. She didn't wait around to be kidnapped here."

Kidnapped. She couldn't even begin to replace that with *murdered*. That was the supposed story. No, Abigail could hardly comprehend her best friend's kidnapping— murder—was far too much.

"Okay," she breathed, standing up. "You stay here. I'm going to call London, and I'm going online. There has got to be a mistake."

She rushed to her room, and opened her laptop.

Savannah Thompson Osaka she typed, and clicked on the news link.

The news was spelled out in pixels. And a jpg. A green-tinted surveillance video of a man with his head covered carrying a woman with a hat onto a train. Abigail clicked on the photograph and enlarged it. Fuzzy as it was, the petite nose and rounded cheek peeping out from under the hat from this angle was easily Savannah's.

She collapsed on the floor with a bang, hitting her knee on the frame of the futon, dropping her laptop.

Saori was there in an instant, looking around the doorway and into the room, then coming to Abigail's side.

"No . . . no . . . no . . ."

Saori's arm was around her then, rocking her, and they stayed like that for a long time.

CHAPTER 14

Abigail leaned over to look through the tinted window of The C's private car and to give a half-hearted wave goodbye before it took off with Saori. As the car drove away, Abigail searched her surroundings for anything suspicious, then ran barefoot back inside the apartment building, hurrying through the main door and into her own apartment, making eye contact with the security guard as she shut the door. Thank goodness she was not on the second story . . . the extra steps up the stairs would take too long, and the idea of running into someone else in the stairwell was unbearable.

She locked the door immediately, then rushed through her apartment closing and locking every window and turning on all the lights. She sat cross-legged on her *tatami* floor and grabbed for her phone, scrolling through the contacts for someone to call.

Cheryl. Every time she came across Cheryl's name in her contacts, she thought about deleting it, but could never bring herself to close that chapter in her life by the press of a button. She had Cheryl's phone number back in Canada, but it was some ungodly hour and it would just make Cheryl feel helpless to be so far away, much as Abigail felt now.

She continued scrolling through names of far-away friends and colleagues: Derek. Eduardo. Jess. John. Linda. London.

London! Of course, London! She could go to his hotel now—not wait until tomorrow—and be protected by its walls and his arms.

"Abigail?" he answered, dazed, when she dialed his number.

"Yeah, it's me. Something awful—"

His voice was suddenly clear.

"Are you okay, Abigail? Are you all right?"

"I'm safe. For now. But Savannah—" Her voice caught. "I can't be alone. Can I come over? Please?"

"Stay right there. I'm coming to get you."

And with that, he hung up. She calculated how long it would be until he arrived, and it was too long. Every second she was alone, unsafe, despairing, was too long. She should have gone in Saori's car. She could have asked the security guard outside her door to take her to The C. But who was he?

She could trust London, that she knew.

In her contacts, Savannah's name blazed clearly.

Savannah, with her strawberry curls and perfect teeth was alive and well on the screen of Abigail's phone.

She can't be gone, she insisted, trying to reassure herself. *Here she is, right here.*

She pressed the CALL button and stared at the image a moment longer, as tears welled in her eyes.

Moshi, moshi! Savannah no keitai desu. Messegi o shite onegai shimasu.

The message continued and the tears made their way over the lids of her eyes and down her cheek. She had been so self-obsessed that fear had been overriding the fact that her friend was actually gone. No, not *gone*, nor missing anymore, but actually dead.

Dead. The word resonated in her mind. Death had not been something real for her in a very long time. During her five years in Japan, her grandmother had passed away, but death is a little different when you're living so far away from the person you've lost.

Abigail leaned against her wall, only now noticing that her blouse was moist from tears, but she didn't care and wiped at her face haphazardly. She remembered the first time she returned home after her grandmother had died and visited the grave. She'd brought a box of tissues in preparation for the waterworks, as she and her grandmother had been very close, but no tears came. She felt no connection between the cold graveyard and the warmth of her grandmother. Perhaps it was because she didn't have the memory of a funeral, full of emotion. In fact, she'd been sitting in the same spot when her mother called her with the news and this place was a more significant connection with her passing than the cemetery where her body rested.

Would the kitchen table be the connection with Savannah's death? Would she ever be able to drink Chinese flower tea again without breaking down?

She pressed the CALL button again.

"Pick up, Savannah, come on! Saori just heard wrong. Please, Savannah!"

Just then, she heard a click, followed by shuffling.

"Oh! Savannah! I'm so damn relieved, Savannah!"

Tears came quicker than before. She stood up in excitement, pacing the room. She felt as if she could explode.

On the other end of the line, though, she could not hear Savannah's voice. In place of the voice she needed to hear were muffled voices—two men—but she couldn't make out any words. Not timbre, language, distance, nor intention, and in moments the line disconnected.

She looked around the room in confusion and in fear. Who had answered the phone? She paced nervously through her apartment. She could not sit still, nor could she think straight.

Savannah was an independent woman like herself, and Abigail had never worried about her because she knew Savannah could take care of herself. But if this could happen to Savannah, it could certainly happen to Abigail.

The thought stopped Abigail's pacing in front of her kitchen table. She looked down at it to see the corner of the letter from English World, rumpled from when she'd stuffed it in her pocket, smoothed from taking it out again and dropping it on the table.

She reached for it tentatively. *Perhaps London was right about me leaving for a while.* All she needed to do was phone the number for an authorization code. They could have a ticket waiting for her at the airport whenever she wanted to leave.

It would also prove to London—and herself—that she could take care of herself without his money. This

way she could show him that she hadn't been unreason-
able the other night. She knew what measures to take,
and when. And now, with things dangerous here in
Japan, skipping out for a while would be best. She had
already closed the schools . . . her responsibilities no
longer obligated her to stay.

She picked up the phone and dialed the number on
the letter. *Perhaps the person on the other line will be able
to answer some of my questions. Maybe they can tell me if
Savannah ever received her authorization code.*

But there was no person on the other end, only a lifeless recorded voice prompting her.

*Thank you for calling. For privacy purposes, this call is
not recorded. At the tone, state your name.*

English. Had none of the Japanese staff received this
offer?

Please state your name.

"Oh, um, Abigail."

After a short pause, "I'm sorry. 'Ohum Abigail' is not
a valid entry. Please state your name again."

She spoke her full name, slowly this time.

"Thank you. Please state your postal code."

"Four-five-six-zero-zero-five-one."

"Thank you. Please enter the five-digit code at the
bottom of your offer letter on your keypad."

After following the prompts, the mechanical voice
awarded Abigail with the confirmation code with an
entire lack of enthusiasm.

"Would you like to leave Tuesday, Wednesday, or
Thursday?"

Those were the only options—today, tomorrow, or the day after? That wasn't even enough time to pack! *But I suppose if they believe I am in danger, the sooner I leave Japan, the better, and of course, it's only temporary.*

"Tomorrow."

"For the safety of your colleagues, students and yourself, please keep this information absolutely confidential. Bring your confirmation code to Nagoya International Airport and check-in at the Kankouku-Hawaii Travel station to receive your physical ticket. Once again, for your safety and that of others, please keep this information absolutely confidential."

Without a goodbye, the phone disconnected. *What a strange process.* She looked at the phone number again and noticed the country code suggested the number wasn't even based in Japan. What was that code? South Korea?

A loud knock at her door startled her. In front of her, her phone displayed her recent calls–the cold mechanical number and the two to Savannah. What if malicious voices behind Savannah's phone had tracked her phone to this apartment?

The knock came louder and more urgently. Abigail grabbed for a butcher's knife in the kitchen. Guns were illegal here in Japan, so she had a fighting chance with a knife. She placed her back against the kitchen wall so that she could jump out at her attackers when they came down the hallway.

She could hear the door handle rattling, and then another knock, this time accompanied by a booming, urgent voice.

"Abigail! Are you there?"

She couldn't remember a time that she had been so relieved to hear a man's voice. It was London, here to save her! "Oh! London! Yes, yes, yes! Just a sec!"

She placed the knife down on the kitchen counter and rinsed her face quickly. The letter on the table caught her eye and she stuffed it in her kimono pocket, then ran to open the door, first looking through the peephole.

The moment the door opened, the two fell into each other's arms and stayed there a moment.

"London, it's Savannah . . ."

He held her body close to his and ran his hand against her back, "Shh . . . I know. I looked it up on the way here."

Abigail was sobbing now, glad to have London's support to keep her from collapsing. "Can . . . can we stay in the hotel tonight? I don't want to be here."

His hand traced its way down her body and he lifted her like a child. She buried her face in his chest. She could hear the door close behind them and the muffled inquiries of her French neighbor before she gave way to exhaustion.

❧

The softness of the bed on her bare skin contrasted sharply with the ache inside her head when the sun awoke her. London lay beside her, just as bare, staring at her.

"Thank you for coming last night." Abigail forced the first words from her still-sleepy vocal chords.

He kissed her head gently and smiled. "I would come for you anytime."

Abigail sat up. She had never considered loyalty as one of the traits she desired in a relationship; it had simply never occurred to her. But she found London's dedication just what she needed from him now.

London slipped off the edge of the bed and the light from the windows played with the angles of his body before he slipped on some silky boxers.

"Would you like some breakfast?"

"Just some orange juice would be great."

The last night still seemed so unreal. She could not wrap her mind around the green-tinted surveillance images of her friend being carried through Tokyo's subway system, where they had taken some of their first photos in Japan together. *Maybe I can bring some photos of Savannah tonight to the travel company to see if they recognize her, if she got the ticket.*

"Oh! London!" She could not see him, but could hear him in the kitchen with the water running. She slipped out of the bed and looked around the floor for her clothes. When she gave up she wrapped the sheet around her and headed toward the kitchen.

"London, I took your advice," she started as she turned the corner.

London was standing over the table with a piece of crumpled paper in his hands. On the table, Abigail's clothes were clean and pressed and her phone was placed neatly on top. *That must be the English World offer.*

"Oh, you found it already! I'm going to leave the country for a while like you suggested. You were right. It's far too dangerous here right now. Plus, I need some time to fully grasp . . . you know, everything. With Savannah."

"English World is giving you an all-expenses paid vacation to Hawaii?"

Abigail could tell that London was not as happy about this as she'd hoped.

"London, I wouldn't call it a vacation. It's a way to stay safe for a while. They're worried that I could be a target. Isn't this exactly what you were trying to do only days ago?" She was still emotionally drained and her temper was short.

"English World is harming their students and their employees, but they can pay for you to go to Hawaii? You won't let me take care of you, but you'll let a company that can't even take care of their employees take care of you? If English World would spend this money on their schools, maybe students like Atsushi wouldn't be attacking teachers in the street."

Tears welled up in Abigail's eyes. She had done this partially for him and he was attacking her for English World's mistakes the same way he'd attacked her the day they met. "Throwing a thousand dollars at a school isn't going to save the company, but it could save a person's life! It could have saved Savannah's life!"

She held back her tears and walked up to London, keeping eye contact, and snatched the paper from his hand, folding it up neatly. "If you'll excuse me, I need to get back to my apartment to pack. I'm leaving tonight."

She dressed in silence. London watched her with a mix of fire and regret in his eyes.

"I'm leaving tonight. This is supposed to be confidential, so please keep it so. I can call you when I'm settled, and when I'm not so angry, so we can try to talk this over."

London stayed silent, but gathered her up in his arms. His lips pressed against hers, and she didn't struggle. London walked Abigail to one of the hotel cars.

"Please use this car to go to the airport, too. I don't want you using the train that late at night."

CHAPTER 15

She'd never been on such a small plane. This was the kind of commuter plane businessmen took from Nagoya to Tokyo, or San Diego to Los Angeles. Of course, this was probably a little nicer. More like something they'd take if their company owned the plane.

The thought ran through Abigail's mind: Did English World own this plane? Did they still own planes?

"Excuse me," she said to the flight attendant, stopping her as she passed with drinks. "Is this airplane owned by English World, the Japanese company?"

The attendant, a petite Korean woman barely twenty years old, smiled and shook her head. "No, ma'am. It is from South Korea, not Japan. English World has had ticket-holders on this plane in the past, but as far as I know they do not own it."

"It's so small."

"Not to worry. It is not very small, just smaller than you may be familiar with."

"True. It's no Singapore Air—that's what I take when I go from Japan home to California, and vice versa. That's a huge plane. Very comfortable, though."

"Are you comfortable now?"

"Oh, yes, yes. I suppose I'm just a little nervous."

"It is very safe, ma'am. And Kauai is not far now."

Abigail considered that she might not be so nervous about the flight so much as what lay at the other end of it. Supposedly a driver hired by English World would meet her to take her to her hotel. He wouldn't be holding a sign with her name, though; they wanted to be as safe and careful as possible. The driver would be holding a pineapple, of all things, and that was how she'd recognize him.

She drummed her fingers against the faux-leather armrest.

Ah, pineapple. Her mind flashed back to London placing a square in her mouth and instructing her on the finer points of enjoying the fruit of his island.

Would he be in Nagoya when she returned? And how soon would she be back? The return ticket was open-ended, so she assumed she could leave when she felt safe, though it would make sense to wait until the murderer had been caught.

Poor Savannah. Had she been here? Had she been on a plane, maybe this plane, on her way to Hawaii? Just to come back too soon—maybe she saw that Amy Hart took luggage, too, and assumed as Abigail had that folks weren't being kidnapped, but leaving per English World's offers.

Or had she never gotten that far at all? Had she been kidnapped before leaving, planning to see Abigail before she left? It wouldn't take much threatening to convince someone to call family and say you're somewhere you're not. And what went through her mind then—knowing she was so close to safety, and yet so far?

Which was worse? Having safety and leaving it under misapprehensions, or being so close to safety you could almost touch it . . . but not quite?

Abigail wiped her eyes with the back of her hand and inhaled deeply. She'd have who knew how long, maybe weeks, to mourn. This was not the time. She needed to get to Kauai, get to her hotel, and then . . . relax into her grief. Into the knowledge that she should have been meeting Savannah here for a vacation in the tropics with her best friend.

"Macadamia nuts and something to drink, ma'am?" the flight attendant asked, snapping her out of herself.

"No thanks. Wait. Yes, I will have some macadamia nuts."

Abigail chomped on the sweet nuts, feeling their thickness on her teeth. She focused on the taste and sensation, if only to avoid thinking about Savannah.

This is how London would want me to taste these, she thought.

Abigail hadn't brought much luggage. She hadn't needed much. And the plane was so small that it didn't even have a baggage machine. A couple of husky guys simply unloaded the plane's contents onto a half dozen carts and wheeled them to the disembarking area. Abigail spotted her red suitcase immediately at the bottom of one cart and waited patiently for the other passengers to remove their bags.

When she could finally free her suitcase, she turned around, only to stop in her tracks.

"You've got to be kidding me," she muttered.

He hadn't seen her yet, buried as he was in his coffee and book. His blond curls hung tousled, and he hadn't shaved, at least not in a day or so. His tank top and cargo shorts were wrinkled, and she noticed he rubbed his eyes now and then.

She neared him without trying to draw his attention during her approach.

"London?"

His head snapped up, and his book snapped shut. "Abigail! You're here!"

"Yes, and, for some reason, so are you."

"I wasn't sure what time you'd be here. Your flight must have been through an independent company, because I couldn't get any info at all. And Cranes can always get whatever info they want. They were very private about you, though. Made me nervous. I got here several hours ago. Did you just arrive?"

He looked at her bag and leaned over to grab the handle for her.

"Leave it," she commanded. "What are you doing here?"

His aqua eyes searched her dark ones, as though he were trying to figure out if she could possibly not be happy to see him.

"What do you mean? You were coming here, and I didn't want to leave it how we did. Besides, Hawaii is my home state and I want to show it off. I told you I don't surf, but I can take you out for a kayak tour, show you some sea turtles, escort you around the pineapple plantations, we can climb volcanoes . . . all the touristy stuff. I'm looking forward to being your host, like you were mine."

"What are you saying, London? We're not on vacation here. I'm hiding out, and trying to grieve the loss of my friend! Plus, I have a place to stay and a ride to get there."

Abigail saw out of the corner of her eye a tall, bulky man in dark slacks and collared shirt holding a pineapple awkwardly under his arm.

"I don't understand exactly why you have to go where English World sets you up. I mean, you're here."

"Just let it be, London. I'll be back in Japan when this has all blown over."

"Let me keep you safe here."

Abigail stepped away from him. "For goodness sakes, London, how many times did you tell me not to worry about you and your money and your plans? Like you, I, too, am an adult who can make her own choices. And if I'm making a mistake, well, hell, it's my mistake to make!"

London stood, and she noticed how ragged he looked. How long had he been sitting here waiting for her? How soon after she left his hotel had he gone to the airport to be sure he made it here in time to meet her? In time to tell her what he wanted her to do, and wrap it up all pretty as though it were a vacation they'd decided together that they'd take.

She turned on her heels, and walked swiftly away.

"Abigail!" he called after her, and she looked around at the travelers now watching with interest.

He jogged up next to her just as she reached the driver.

"Abigail! Are you going to let your smug pride come before—"

But he was cut off by the driver, who asked in a deep baritone, "Abigail Dennis?"

"Yes," she said as he took her luggage.

London stepped between them. He was trimmer than the driver, but just as tall, possibly taller, and he blocked the driver's view.

"Come with me. Abigail, don't let your pride—"

He started again and was cut off again, this time by the driver stepping to the side and rolling her luggage out the door toward his car, a black SUV with tinted windows.

"I have to go now. We'll talk when this is all over."

London folded his arms across his chest. Abigail thought he might have reached his breaking point. "Will we?"

"Yes."

"We'll see."

"I'll see you in Nagoya?"

"We'll see," he repeated, and turned to walk back to his own luggage, abandoned where he'd been sitting.

❧

The car rolled along, not rushing to its destination. Abigail leaned her head on the window and watched the scenery pass. The verdant rainforest they passed grew so thick in spaces that beams of sunlight through the leafy treetops were few and far between. Her heart ached, her throat burned, as she fought back the tears.

Everything had been going according to plan; Abigail was to be safe here and London was to be waiting at home when she returned.

"But then he returns to his Alpha Male ways and shows up here, ignoring the many times I've told him the importance to me of making my own decisions," she whispered under her breath.

She felt somehow betrayed by this man she'd come to love too quickly, whom she'd judged to be honest and respectful. He'd turned out to be nothing but a controlling lover. Hadn't she made it this far in life without allowing herself to be drawn to a possessive man wearing the thin guise of protector? Hadn't she had solid years of being strong, of being the woman she wanted to be?

As the car turned onto a dirt road, everything around her rumbled as the vehicle bounced over the rough path. The forest grew thicker still until suddenly it opened into a wide expanse of green fields. She studied through the tinted window the plants that grew there, still green with infancy. Pineapples, she realized, and her mind shot back to London, his fingers dripping with pineapple juice as he placed the flesh of the fruit between her lips.

What had he wanted to say when he was cut off? Twice. Don't let her pride get in the way of . . . her safety?

Her time away from work? Their relationship? Their . . . love?

He'd shut down then, when she insisted he let her make her decisions. No, it was when she insisted he let her make her own mistakes. Was he still worried about her? Or was he just sick of her pride?

He'd crossed his arms. Abigail knew how to read body language cues; she was a teacher, after all. And a closed body reflected a closing of the mind to the situation. He'd implied he might not be waiting for her when she returned.

"I can't blame him," she muttered, but then shot a glance at the driver, hoping he hadn't heard. His eyes were glued to the dirt road stretching before them.

She couldn't expect him to wait forever, and maybe they just weren't right for each other. He wanted someone he could control, and she wanted to be in control of her own destiny. It had been a relationship made only for a season. Romantic moments clouding her judgment. Tender words bolstering her pride during a rough patch in life. And, of course, the sex.

Abigail saw a speak of a house on the horizon far in the distance, and she kept her eyes on it as it grew larger and closer.

The sex, the mind-blowing sex. They'd connected there, and it could have made anyone believe they were made to be together.

Her eyes burned again, tears threatening. It had to be more than physical, what they'd had, the time they'd spent together. It simply had to be. How could she have been so wrapped up in and so surrendered to something that was only sexual?

The house became defined as it grew larger. A two-story plantation-style house, painted white with cream trim like frosting, tinted windows to keep the sun and heat out of the house, and a wrap-around porch.

"Is this where I'm staying?" she asked the driver, hopeful. The house looked like a cloud of comfort and safety, far away from the crazy world.

"Yes, ma'am."

"Is it a working pineapple plantation?"

"Yes, ma'am."

She'd get to taste fresh pineapple after all. Abigail smiled for the first time in what felt like forever.

Her smile dropped suddenly when figures sitting on rocking chairs on the porch came into view. Who would she be staying with, after all?

"Who is that there . . . ?" she started.

When the car finally pulled to a stop, the driver exited without a word. Abigail reached for the door handle and found the childproof locks engaged. She tapped on the window, but the driver was removing her luggage.

She felt trapped, and dread seeped into her pores. She banged on the window.

"Hey! Hey, let me out!"

The driver opened the door calmly and stepped aside as Abigail bolted from the car.

"What the heck were you thinking?"

"I'm sorry. I should have opened the door before unloading the luggage."

"No—you shouldn't have locked me in!"

He looked at her, puzzled.

"You," she started, suddenly unsure of the situation, "you had the childproof locks on the doors."

"Oh, my . . . I am so sorry. I didn't realize."

"Well, you should turn them off."

"I will. I will. Now, let me show you to your hosts."

Abigail eyed him suspiciously and grabbed the handle for her luggage. "I'll take this myself. Now, what hosts? I thought English World just sent me here. I didn't know I was to be meeting anyone."

Now that Savannah is gone, she added, but not aloud.

"That was for their protection. You're not the only one who was given the offer of leaving Japan."

He led the way toward the house and Abigail looked around them, taking in the gorgeous plantation grounds, before adjusting her view toward the porch. She stopped short when she made out who the people on the porch were, these hosts of hers.

"It can't be."

There in a rocking chair on the porch, rocking gently, a beer in hand, smiling wide, was Mr. Inudori, CEO of English World. Abigail had never seen him in person, but she had met briefly the person rocking next to him and drinking a tall glass of juice: Mr. Toru Ito, VP of English World. They'd been introduced at a dinner for executives two and a half years ago, when he'd sat across from Abigail, who was a new administrative head at the time, taking in her first executives' dinner. She'd been flattered by Mr. Ito's prodding for more information on her pedagogy theory, but she judged later that he'd just been polite and she really ought not to have gotten on a soapbox at such an event.

Abigail left her luggage at the bottom of the stairs and climbed to the porch in shock. She felt as though she were looking at ghosts.

"This is Ms. Abigail Dennis," Mr. Toru Ito announced, standing and helping Mr. Inudori to his feet. Inudori looked old and weak next to the sturdy, middle-aged Ito. "She is the one I mentioned. I consider Ms. Dennis to be a very smart woman."

The heat rose in Abigail's cheeks.

"I see. Ms. Dennis. I am very happy to know you accepted our offer."

She shook Mr. Inudori's extended hand, a delicate thing, something that might be crushed if she squeezed with an ounce of firmness. No, she decided, his hand wasn't delicate. His handshake was. This CEO was playing gentle, but she felt authority in his hands.

Mr. Ito extended a hand, and Abigail shook that, too.

He looked her over, making her feel exposed. "I did not know if you would come. But I am happy you did. You look very well. Many people are so weary from this difficult time with English World, but you look very well."

"Thank you . . ."

Her words were hesitant, guarded. Why were they here? Why was she here? Why had they been talking about her?

"Please sit," the CEO offered in a tone that carried a hint of command. He motioned at an empty chair near Mr. Ito. "What will you drink?"

"What?"

"What will you drink?"

"Oh, I'm all right," she lied. In fact, she was parched, a combination of the heat and humidity and the ghosts on the porch. These men were not dead! These men had not been kidnapped!

"No," he argued, then commanded, "have a drink."

"Well . . ."

Toru spoke up then, and Abigail wondered how it could be that he remembered her. How it could be that he had thought to mention her to the CEO and suggest he bring her here?

"Beer," Toru ordered the attendant standing suddenly in the doorway. "Or do you like wine?"

"No, no alcohol." She had to keep her mind straight. Guarded as she was, she had the feeling it was right to be guarded. "What is that you're drinking?"

"POG juice. It contains pineapple juice, orange juice, and guava juice. A drink of Hawaii."

"I'll have that, please."

The attendant moved back into the house with her order.

Toru Ito pulled the rocking chair to his right closer to his. "Please sit down, Ms. Abigail Dennis."

"Just Abigail is fine."

"Sit down, Abigail," Mr. Inudori offered, again in a way that felt like a command.

Abigail moved silently to sit down, instantly regretting that she'd let him tell her what to do. Were these still her bosses? She wasn't quite sure, and so she wasn't sure if she ought to feel offended.

"She does not talk so much as you said, Toru."

"The last time I met her, she talked very much. All night. As I told you, she had many ideas for the school and teaching. Very passionate."

The ghosts on the porch spoke of her as though she were the ghost.

Mr. Inudori rocked forward and looked around the VP to Abigail. "Toru says you have passion for teaching."

"Yes."

"Your city is . . ."

"Nagoya."

"The Nagoya schools have been open all this time?"

Toru Ito answered for her. "Yes, they have. Very good scheduling, Abigail."

"I have a good staff." Abigail thought of Saori's late nights. Then she thought of London Crane's golden curls falling into his eyes as he leaned down to kiss her.

"So modest."

"The parents and students are not that happy, though. And the power is being turned off—we were going to hold lectures." She was getting off-topic. "I'm sorry, but I must ask before we go any further: What is happening here?"

Toru answered with a laugh first, before speaking.

"We are relaxing in rocking chairs at the most beautiful house at the most beautiful pineapple plantation in all of Kauai. And here is your juice."

"But all the newspapers at home show you both as missing. Maybe kidnapped."

"And perhaps murdered?"

"Yeah, and here you are, perfectly safe."

Mr. Inudori rocked forward again, with a smile. "You sound disappointed! Toru will not like to hear that," he said and nudged the man next to him.

"Not disappointed," she confirmed, "just confused."

Toru Ito answered this time. "We were worried that people were upset about the school's financial issues. This is a safe place. This is the same reason we have offered to bring you here."

Abigail drank down the sticky-sweet juice, soothing her dry throat, before continuing. "But what about the CFO and Amy Hart? And what happened to Richard Mulrooney, and—"

Her voice caught in her throat. She couldn't even say Savannah's name aloud. Her eyes burned, and she stood, walking to the edge of the stairs, hoping they wouldn't see her get emotional.

"We asked them to come here to be safe, too. Mr. Yamamoto and Ms. Hart are safe here, and we have many people coming, from Sapporo and Mito and Yokohama. Ms. Hart is up the stairs. Do you want to see her? I think she is napping, though. She was very busy with her schools, and all she wants to do here is nap and eat and read and nap more. A very good vacation for her."

"And the others?"

Toru shook his head. "This is why we came here. This is why we brought you here. This is why I am glad you took our offer."

"What happened?"

"They," Mr. Inudori cut in, "did not accept our offer. Very sad. We cannot make someone safe if they do not want to be safe."

Toru Ito stood with her and wrapped an arm around her shoulder. Abigail shuddered; this felt too much like the last train of the night, but, looking around, she saw she had no escape route.

"I know Ms. Savannah Thompson was your friend. I am sorry."

"Where did you say Amy Hart was?"

"Ms. Hart is up the stairs in her room."

"I'd like to see her." Without another word, Abigail squirmed free and showed herself into the house.

From behind her she could hear the CEO laugh and tease the VP in Japanese, "She doesn't much like you, Toru."

CHAPTER 16

Abigail stood looking from one to the other of the only two closed doors upstairs. Finally, she chose one at random and hoped it was Amy Hart's. She had a fifty percent chance of being correct. Otherwise, it would be Yoshikazu Yamamoto, the CFO, and she was done with executives for the moment. Done with ghosts.

It was Amy Hart who answered Abigail's knock.

"Hello? What time is it?" she asked as she opened the door.

She was rubbing her eyes sleepily and was wearing a faded designer t-shirt and jean shorts. When she saw Abigail, she squinted, processing.

"You must be . . . um . . . Dennis? Abigail Dennis?"

"Yes, and you're Amy. We met at a meeting in Tokyo once, just once."

"Yeah, there are always a lot of people at those meetings. Glad that's over. Won't you come in?"

"Sure." She followed Amy. It was a good-sized room with a bathroom en suite, but nothing like London's posh hotel. "What do you mean, it's all over?"

Amy stretched her arms over her head, extending her already tall and lean figure. "Over. You know, the school's done with."

"But you've been keeping yours open. I didn't know you'd given up."

"I wanted to hold out hope. I said it was for the teachers, but hell, I had a lot of credit card debt, student loan debt from college . . . I couldn't just write off the money they owed me. So I guess I just hoped they'd fix whatever had gone wrong with the company." She examined Abigail. "You stayed a long time, too. Same reason?"

"No . . ."

And Abigail realized she'd told her reasons for staying so many times they were becoming trite. And in light of the reasons Amy gave, hers would sound self-important and idealistic.

But it turned out Amy hadn't wanted to hear her answer, really. She simply shrugged and returned to her queen-sized bed. She began straightening the quilt over the top and then stopped.

"I forgot. They have a maid. So used to living in my own apartment. You'll like it here, Abigail Dennis. They take care of us."

"I don't really need—"

"Oh, come now, everyone wants to be taken care of a little."

"Well, I'm pretty independent."

"I'm not saying let them boss you around. I'm saying let them take care of you."

Abigail sighed. If she wanted to be taken care of, she'd have let London do it more often. And Amy Hart was beginning to get annoying.

Amy sat on the mattress and grabbed a brush off the mahogany night stand. She motioned with the brush to the wicker chair next to the bed.

"Have a seat, Abigail. Relax a while. That's what this place is all about. And God knows, we need it. God knows, we deserve it."

Abigail sat down. "Relaxing, huh? Haven't had much of that since English World started to have issues."

"Yeah, but the plantation's all about it. Seriously." She ran the brush through her fine long hair and said, "I sleep until whenever I want, maybe until ten, then have them bring breakfast to my room. I take a long bath, do some reading, maybe take a nap. I guess it's good there's no internet here—I'd be on Twitter all day and people would think I was a lazy bum when I tweeted about what I was up to. I do miss it, though. I haven't heard from anyone since I got here."

"It's odd that there's no internet." Abigail realized that when she'd said goodbye to London, it might have really been more concrete than she'd wanted. She had assumed she'd be able to email a quick note to say she was safe. And, who knew, maybe she'd even apologize. But now there was no chance to do even that.

"They want to keep us safe. That's the whole point of this place. Oh, and relaxation. So when I get hungry I go down for lunch. They cook real good here. Real good. I might have a rock on the patio afterwards and talk to the big wigs, or maybe hang out in here."

"They don't . . . *expect* anything from you?" Abigail asked, a chill running down her spine as she pictured Toru Ito wrapping his arm around her shoulders.

"Expect? No, not really."

"Well, that's good."

Amy started to speak again, then paused in her thoughts.

"You know, now that you ask, I guess there is one thing they expect."

Abigail just looked at her, raised eyebrows urging Amy to continue.

"We all have to have dinner together at six. Mr. Inudori, Mr. Ito, Mr. Yamamoto and me. You'll have to, too. And I think they said more administrative heads are coming from Sapporo and Mito and Yokohama. They'll be there, too. It's a big, fancy dinner, every night. And we work the entire time. I think that's why they spread it out so long. To get more work out of us." She squished her nose in mock distaste.

"What work? I thought we were here to be safe. And relax, as you say."

"Well, they do need our input for the planning and everything. I mean, that's why they picked who they did to come. People they thought would have good input. So we brainstorm there, flesh out ideas."

Amy shook her hair over her shoulders and set down the brush. She stood up and went to a sliding glass door in the back of the room. "Wanna go on the balcony? The view's great at sunset, and we're almost there. It's the prettiest thing you'll ever see."

Abigail felt uneasy again, and, despite everything, unsafe, too. Her habit overcame her, and she pressed a hand to the back of her neck.

"Amy, what planning? I haven't heard about plans for anything."

"Didn't you speak with them downstairs when you came? They told me before they showed me to my room."

"We talked for a few minutes and then I showed myself in. I wanted to see you. I haven't even been to my room."

"You wanted to see me? How lovely!" She stretched again, a tabby cat, all peaches and cream. She gave the distinct impression that her nap had either just concluded or had been interrupted.

"What plan, Amy?" Abigail asked again, coming around the bed and joining her next to the door.

Amy slid the door open, and a gust of warm, pineapple-spiced air drifted around them.

"Well," she hesitated, "now I don't know if I should say. Maybe they want to tell you."

"Are they re-opening the schools?" Even as she said it, she was more doubtful than hopeful.

"In a way—"

There was a knock on the door, startling Abigail but not Amy.

"Come in!" she called in a sing-song voice.

An attendant peeked in and nodded to the women.

"Mr. Inudori would like to take dinner early. Will the two of you join us in fifteen minutes in the dining hall?"

"Of course. I was feeling ready to call down for a little snack, so an early dinner is good news. Now, Abigail, please. You must relax. You're not at work anymore."

Abigail looked Amy over. She'd remembered her as a tightly-wound, if not a bit egotistical, colleague. But this easy-breezy woman was altogether new. How would Abigail herself be after a week of relaxation? Secretly, she hoped she'd be less like Amy Hart and more . . . more what? More, perhaps, as she was on the rooftop with London.

She shook her head, bringing herself back to the present situation. London was on his way back to Japan. Or Maui. The tea set was tucked away in the pantry at her apartment in Nagoya, gathering dust. The roof of the school hadn't had a visitor since Abigail turned the key to lock the door. Certainly the power had been turned off at the main school and office by now, too.

"Just tell me about the plan. I'll act surprised when they tell me, all right?"

As Abigail had anticipated, Amy Hart couldn't resist spilling the secret.

"Okay. Come back inside and shut the sliding door. Don't want them to hear me tell you. But you have to act surprised later. That's probably why we're having dinner early, so they can tell you."

Amy settled back on the mattress and patted the spot next to her, as though they would be gossiping like schoolgirls.

"So . . . you know how English World is going under? Well, it has *gone* under, I mean. The coffers are empty, as they say. But how did they get empty so quick, right? Mr. Inudori says what was happening with this bad economy was not enough students were signing up, and too much money was going out. Remember a while back when it seemed like every paycheck was a week late? That was the start."

Abigail remembered, and that experience had been the reason she'd stuck with English World more recently. They'd always come through then, sent the paychecks. It was only recently they'd stopped honoring their commitments.

Amy continued, "Mr. Inudori had the foresight to see the school was going down. So instead of let it slow-leak its way to the bottom and die, he started setting aside some money, just a little here and there. That made it sink faster, but with a bigger nest egg saved up, a new venture could really take off."

"So he's planning to re-open the schools." Abigail wasn't sure it was legal or honest, and it certainly hadn't been fair to the teachers, but at least the end result might be good. The end justifying the means, and all that.

"That's the kicker. Not the English World schools." Amy leaned in close. "New schools. Ones they won't track as having used the little bits siphoned off from English World. They're going to open schools in South Korea, and they are going to make us all rich."

Abigail stood suddenly and began pacing the floor. Amy remained perched on the bed, a puzzled look on her face.

"Wait. Are you upset about this?"

"Yes!" Abigail exclaimed, not stopping her pacing.

"Well, I just don't get why you'd be so upset."

"Th—the students—" she stuttered through her anger.

"No one is forced to go to school there. No one is forced to pay in advance for something. At English World, yes, but they could have gone to other schools. Month-by-month schools."

"And the teachers?" Abigail stopped pacing finally and turned to Amy, hands on her hips.

"Again, no one forced them to stay. They could have left the minute they didn't get a paycheck." Amy stood up then, laying a gentle hand on Abigail's shoulder. "And if you're worried about your paycheck, don't be. They will not only be compensating us *well* in Korea, they'll also be giving us higher positions."

"*That's* why they brought us here?"

"Yeah."

"Not to keep us safe?"

"Well, maybe. I mean, some people are upset over there, right? But mainly I think they wanted to bring their *best talent* here to start the new schools . . . Abigail, wait!"

She'd stormed out of the room, and was heading down the stairs. Amy Hart rushed out after her.

"Don't tell them I told you! They wanted to tell you at dinner, I think!"

"Oh, I'll tell them . . . I'll tell them what I think of their dishonest . . ." she stomped down a stair with each word, ". . . illegal plan!"

Abigail found Mr. Inudori and Toru Ito on the porch still.

"Oh, is it dinner now?" Toru asked her, getting up lazily from his chair, not removing his eyes from Abigail.

But he was focusing on her body and not her face, and thus not registering her fury.

Amy rushed out on to the patio and grabbed Abigail's arm in an attempt to stay her words.

"I might have mentioned the Korea plan to Abigail, Mr. Inudori! I thought you'd already told her. She's upset about it."

Mr. Inudori exchanged glances with Toru.

"Oh?" he asked, more to the VP than to Amy.

"Maybe she did not explain everything correctly," Toru offered, and moved toward Abigail, taking her arm.

Abigail removed it harshly.

"Then explain it *correctly*," Abigail challenged him.

Suddenly she felt a crowd behind her. Looking over her shoulder she saw the driver in all his bulk, and two other men dressed as he was. Behind them stood the CFO, Yoshikazu Yamamoto.

"What is this, Inudori?" he asked, pushing his way out from the bulky men.

"You should ask Toru."

Toru Ito, Abigail suddenly realized, was the youngster of the group, and he shrank back from the confrontation.

"Please. I will talk to her to explain. She will not be upset when she understands."

"I'm *right here!*" Abigail cut in. "And I don't want to be talked into anything. I'd like to go back to Japan."

The three executives exchanged glances before Amy Hart cut in.

"Come on, guys. Let her go home. Rick and Savannah didn't want any part of the new school either, and you let them go. Just let Abigail go, too. More for us. Come on, you only want committed people on the team, right?"

Abigail reeled on her. "Savannah was *here*?"

"Yeah. Didn't you know?"

"When did she leave?"

"Like the day after she arrived. She was on the first plane back to Japan the next morning. Was upset, like you. I mean, I don't get it. But if you can afford to pass this up, then that's your business."

"Savannah—" Abigail choked on her words. Did Amy Hart really think Savannah was back in Osaka, sipping *sake* and looking for a new job?

Toru Ito spoke up, facing Mr. Yamamoto, putting himself between Abigail and the bulk of men.

"I will talk to her."

Abigail could tell something under the words passed between them, but she had no idea what it was.

"Okay. Bring her downstairs."

"Do not harm her!" Toru commanded to the men as the two grabbed Abigail by the arms and wrestled her back in the house.

❧

Abigail wasn't sure if she was more frightened of Toru Ito coming down to "talk to her" or of the widening possibilities of what actually happened to Richard and Savannah.

She looked around the dim room. They had said to take her "downstairs," but it was still part of the main house. A hidden room, Abigail thought when they had exposed the door behind the pantry. One step down, and she was tossed onto exposed dirt. Before she could leap back at the door, it was closed and locked from the outside. The only light came through a slit in the wood, too high on the opposite wall for Abigail to look out. She could not even tell if the light came from a lamp in another room or from the setting sun outside, and she realized she hadn't seen enough of the house to have much of an idea about its layout.

After she'd given up kicking the door, charging it, and shouting through it, Abigail felt around the edge for any give, but there was none. The door was flush with the wall. She then followed the wall to the right, tracing it with her hand, slowly shuffling her feet. She had to know her surroundings, even in the dark.

"Sounds solid, this one," she muttered to herself, hearing a thick thud against the wall when she struck it. "Maybe a bookcase on the other side. Maybe a table."

She pounded the wall above her, and it was just as thick.

After she'd traced each of the four walls, she settled next to the most hollow-sounding one. It didn't lead to the outside; the air on this side was cigar-tinged and too quiet. But it would be the only place she'd be able to hear anything. Plus, if the door directly across were to open, she could easily and suddenly push off from the wall, regardless of being light-blind after the darkness, and charge before the intruder could respond. Any other spot would require her to find her way, avoid the opening door, see where she was going.

She couldn't stay in a poised state of readiness forever, but any scuffing near the door and she'd get ready. And then watch out.

An hour passed.

Then another.

The slit of light on the floor remained in one spot, confirming Abigail's guess that the wall was set against another room and not the outdoors.

Out of nowhere, there were suddenly noises on the other side of the door. Abigail crouched. She could make out voices, two of them, one closer and one further away. There was the scraping of objects being moved.

"Oh, no," a woman's voice muttered.

"What is it?" came the answer.

"We're in trouble."

Abigail held her breath, unsure if she should call for help or wait to pounce.

The second voice came through clearer now; both people were in the pantry. "What? Why?"

"He'll skin us alive . . ."

"Stop being so dramatic. What's the problem?'

"We're out of powdered sugar."

Abigail's stomach flipped. Were these the cooks?

"We'd better not be. Chef will kill us. You were supposed to get some during the last visit to town."

"I thought I did!"

Now there came more scraping as the two looked, and Abigail could hardly believe her ears. They were the kitchen help! And they were worried about ingredients for dessert!

"Oh, thank goodness," came the answer. "It's there, behind the condensed milk."

"For heaven's sake, my heart can't take this. I'm telling you, sometimes I want to move back to town and work somewhere normal. A cafe or something. With all the shenanigans going on around here—"

Abigail then rushed to the door, pounded on it, shouted.

"Help! Please, I'm trapped!"

The voices ceased instantly, then resumed, conversing together so low she couldn't make out the words.

"Please help me! I'm trapped! Please let me out! The door is at the back of the pantry!"

But Abigail heard footsteps rush away and the pantry door close, sealing her off by a second door from any hope of rescue. She kicked the door with such force her toe ached.

"What the hell!" she shouted at them, though knowing all too well that they couldn't hear her. "You *know* I'm here? You know I'm here and you're not doing anything about it!"

She shuffled back across the small room to the opposite wall, fury raging. It was everyone. Everyone here knew she was locked up. No one came to help. Not even the bloody servants! How could *anyone* hear that an innocent person was locked up, then just turn and walk away?

Unless they'd done it before.

"Savannah . . ."

They wouldn't have dared let Savannah go home knowing that she knew, assuming she'd just keep it a secret, Abigail decided. They had too much invested in the scheme.

A sickness settled in the pit of her stomach.

Had she been locked up here, too?

As though on cue, she heard voices enter the room to which she had her back. She almost shouted for help, but caught herself. Who knew who'd be there?

There was a barreling laughter, and the scent of cigars ripened.

"Thank you, Ms. Hart," someone said. "You have many good ideas. I like your idea that we might take the same plans and agendas from our Japan schools—we will save much money on creating a new plan. I do not think we should use the same books from Japan. We do not want any connection that we have back in Japan. We want to use very little money, but it is important that we start new."

"Thank you," Amy replied, and Abigail cringed. "And you know, Abigail Dennis was able to keep her schools open with a very small number of teachers left. You may want to adopt whatever method she used to save money on staff."

"We wanted Ms. Dennis's help with that method, but she does not want to stay."

"You can get into her scheduling system online, you know. It's company property, after all, isn't it?"

That sleazy, selfish bitch. That brown-nosed, greedy . . .

"Please have a cigar, Miss Hart. Cuban. Very hard to get in an American state."

"No, thank you. You always offer after dinner, but surely by now you're used to my preference to avoid smoking. I'll be going to bed now."

"Goodnight. We will talk more, but not about the school, so you do not have to stay in our smoke."

Abigail had to cover her nose and mouth, waving away the smoke seeping into the small space.

"I have one question about that before I go," Amy said tentatively, and Abigail could only hope she would make a case for her freedom.

"I think I know what it is." The voice was Toru's.

"Yeah, I'm sure *you* do." Amy chuckled, bringing Abigail's blood to a boil. "Where *did* you take Abigail Dennis?"

There was a sudden exchange of words; it had to be Yamamoto and Inudori. In Japanese—Amy Hart must have never taken the time to learn the language. Under their breaths they hushed:

I'd forgotten that the room is just there.

Can she hear through?

She must be able to. We will move to the other room.

Wait until this one goes. We don't want her to be concerned.

"Miss Hart, you are a very nice woman to think of your colleague. You do not think we would harm Miss Dennis just because she does not want to move to South Korea? No, we will bring her back to Japan, just like the rest."

Abigail suddenly pounded against the wall. "Hey!" she shouted.

It wasn't clear if Amy heard her shout.

"Did you . . . take her to her room?" Amy asked.

Abigail cried, "No! I'm here! Behind the wall! Help!"

But the men spoke louder, obviously trying to cover her muffled voice.

"No, we do not want her to leave and go into the jungle. It is very dangerous, you know. And we are many kilometers from town. I'm sure she's not happy about it, but we did lock her door."

"Where did you take her?"

Abigail continued to pound, and wished she could see what was happening. Was Amy eyeing the wall suspiciously, and trying to get them to tell her? Or was she only mildly interested, and had she bought the story that Abigail had been placed behind a locked door for her own safety?

"Do not worry. She will rest and tomorrow morning we will put her on a flight back to Japan."

"Like with Savannah and Richard."

"Yes, Ms. Hart."

"Okay. If I'm not already up when you're ready to leave, just give her my regards."

After Amy left the room, Abigail stopped pounding, her fists sore and her heart heavy. The conversation on the other side of the wall dropped in volume and into Japanese. Abigail was thankful for her foresight in learning the language, and while she couldn't catch every word, she understood the content.

Either the CEO or the CFO—she couldn't tell the difference in their choked words—reminded Toru Ito that the holding room was on the other side of the wall, and that they should move to the room down the hall to talk.

"Does she speak Japanese?" asked a low-pitched voice. Abigail pictured the CEO throwing a glance at the wall suspiciously.

"I don't know," Toru answered. "Miss Dennis is very bright, and I would not be surprised. But I have never heard her speak it."

"See here now, Inudori," one said, and Abigail realized this must be the voice of Mr. Yamamoto. "What does it matter? We will speak Japanese and if she hears our words, what will she do? Who will she tell?"

"If something goes wrong . . ."

"It never has."

"She might escape."

"It has never happened before. We will give her the drug on the plane, like the others. But what a pain and expense to fly another one back to Japan! Toru!"

Toru Ito sounded much younger than the others, even timid now.

"Yes, Mr. Yamamoto, sir?"

"Do you realize the position you've put us in by insisting we bring that woman here?"

"She is the best administrative head."

"We were looking not only for the best, but the *best fit* for the job. I fear you've let your groin guide your better judgment. And both have disappointed."

Abigail shuddered.

"Yamamoto!" Mr. Inudori caught him sharply. "Let him alone. He may yet convince Miss Dennis to stay."

"And if not?" Yamamoto challenged.

"Then she will go with the others."

The group then made their way out of the room, much to Abigail's despair. She had heard so much and learned so little, just enough to make her even more afraid.

The others. Savannah and Richard, of course. They hadn't been dropped off in Japan and left alone. They were drugged and murdered, and not by a wayward student as the media suggested.

She watched the door, listening with keen ears for the sound of Toru Ito. He was bigger than she was, but had sounded so timid next to the other executives. She'd charge him with all she had, and she was certain she could knock him down. Escape. If she could take him by surprise.

But he didn't show up. Hours passed, and Abigail's eyelids grew heavy. Finally she couldn't help it any longer, and she pressed her back against the wall, crossed her forearms over her knees, and dropped her head on them.

And she was asleep.

❦

It might have been a dream. That was her first thought. Morning light drenched the room and the scent of cigars had long since dissipated.

But when she lifted her head, her eyes ached from the sunlight for a moment, and when they adjusted, she realized it was a bright lamp.

Held by Toru Ito.

Who stood inches from her, breathing thickly.

She bolted up on weak legs.

"What are you doing here? Let me out!"

"Abigail," he breathed without touching her. "Why do you fight this? It is a very good opportunity. And we can work together. We would work together. I would like that very much. We had such a nice discussion before. I think you might like it, too."

"Let me out, please."

"I cannot do that. They have locked the door. They thought I may let you out."

"Would you have?"

"Maybe. That depends."

"On what?" she tested.

"On . . . if you are willing to convince me."

She didn't need clarity. She knew what he meant from his leer and the way his gaze never stayed on her face. It traced her cheeks, her throat, her shoulders, and down the length of her body.

"Are they going to send me home?"

"Yes."

"Safely?"

He didn't answer right away. He looked over his shoulder and dropped his voice. "You should take their offer. You will physically get to Japan, but . . . you know too many things and I do not think you will make it further than the airport. They have people."

"What people?"

"People who are paid. They will do many things for money. I do not want that to happen to you."

"What?"

". . . Anything."

If she weren't so frightened . . . if he weren't the bad guy . . . she might have felt sorry for the awkward man with what could only be described as a long-standing crush. Who knew? If she'd known how he felt back at the dinner years ago, she might have let him call her. Never knowing what he was capable of.

She touched his forearm, hoping she could stop anything further, but coax information from him nonetheless.

"Will you tell me what will happen? That might convince me to stay. And if I stay," she added, "we might work together. Isn't that what you said? Now, don't lie. But maybe just tell me what they've done in the past."

She'd deliberately used *they* instead of *you*. She knew he was part of it. If not directly responsible, his sins were those of omission—he hadn't stopped it.

Chills ran the length of his arm, and he withdrew it, as though her touch had been too much. But then suddenly his arms were wrapping around her, and he was drawing his face close. She stepped away quickly, but remained gentle.

"Tell me what will happen."

"What will happen if you stay?" His breath quickened.

He's thinking of what he wants to do to me if I stay with him here, she realized, and eyed the lantern in his hand. She could knock him out with it, she decided, if need be.

"If I go."

Toru's face dropped, and he sighed.

"There is a plane owned by our company. Not English World. Our new Korean company. They will act as though you will be flown home, but you will be given a sleeping drug in your drinks on the plane. There is a small landing strip we have used; not Narita International Airport. When you are escorted from the plane, you will be too sleepy to fight. They will kill you right after you've arrived in Japan. You will get back to Japan, but you will be dead in less than an hour. They will leave you somewhere. Make it look like someone attacked you—a teacher or student or something. Won't be hard. They have probably posted bail for that parent who attacked you recently. He will be the prime suspect."

"Is—is that what they've done before?"

"With Richard Mulrooney? And—" he stopped, eyed her. He knew better than to dare.

"Did they hire someone to . . ."

"To escort them. Yes. Both of them. Shoot them right after they leave the plane. Deposit them somewhere where they will be found."

Abigail thought of Savannah's lifeless body being carried into the train, presumably asleep. She backed against the wall.

"No . . . no . . ."

And now she really knew too much. Greed leading to corporate fraud leading to murder. He took a step toward her.

"You will stay with us, then? You will stay with me?"

"I will *not*," she insisted, standing up straight, watching the lantern. "I could never work with *murderers*."

He turned away for a moment, licking his emotional wounds, and when he turned back, a fire flickered behind his eyes, a cold fire. Panic rose in Abigail. The human in Toru Ito was gone. Pure desire was in its place, selfish, consuming.

He stepped toward her, smiling coolly.

Suddenly the door opened. Three husky attendants stood behind Mr. Yamamoto. The foursome blocked the entire doorway.

"Done yet, Ito?" Mr. Yamamoto snapped.

"No. She will not stay."

"Then let's get it over with. The plane is standing by. Red-eye flight."

It's still night, Abigail registered, eyeing the lantern.

"Give me a little time." The words slipped from Toru Ito's tongue like thick oil.

"You have had enough time with her."

"I need a little more time."

"You said she won't be convinced."

"Not to convince."

"You have not done *that* yet? Are you even a man?"

Toru whirled back to face Abigail.

"I am a man."

Yamamoto sighed with tired frustration. "Well, fine. Do what you want and be done. We will wait here so she does not beat you."

The attendants laughed along with Yamamoto, which only spurred Toru's testosterone.

He advanced on her; Abigail dodged him and rushed to the doorway, to the wall of men blocking the doorway. One attendant grabbed her roughly and she could feel her skin bruising under his large hands. A shove and she was in Toru Ito's arms, but he was caught off balance by the force.

That was all Yamamoto needed to lose his temper.

"Toru!" he snapped. "You have had too much time! You should act. You always talk, talk, talk. You must act."

"I will." He pulled Abigail's body close to his own. "Just give me time."

"No, your time is up. Come."

Abigail sighed in relief when his body relaxed into obedience and followed the foursome out the door without looking back.

And then she collapsed onto the floor in tears.

CHAPTER 17

Two hours. She'd be hustled into the car and probably drugged on the spot, since she knew what was to happen. She'd go back to Japan, all right, but for all of an hour of drugged life before it was ended. Perhaps her body would be dumped on a train like Savannah's. They'd found Richard just blocks from his apartment. London would see her name in the paper.

London.

She wept even more heavily. She'd told him to let her make her own mistakes. He'd wanted to protect her. And now that's all she wanted. All she wanted in the world. London to break down these walls and gather her in his strong arms and steal her far, far away. Just to be in his arms again.

"London . . ."

She'd let her smug pride get in the way . . . of everything. Her safety. Their love.

And now London was probably thousands of miles away in Japan, thinking he never wanted to see her again. And that's exactly what would happen. All he'd see was her name in the paper.

Abigail pictured his shoulders from behind; London standing at SunRUs when she was trying to avoid him. She hadn't been able to keep herself from admiring the width of them, the power in the muscles. No, that view only came later, when he'd towered over her, exposed, glorious, all muscles and golden tint. But she'd admired his beauty from the start.

And then there was the night on the rooftop when her view of him shifted. He had depth, and what appealed to him about her was something more than looks. He'd examined her in stolen glances, but his words had spoken about the "trust that surrounded her."

Ha. Trust. She'd only gone so far in her trust. It was easy to trust a big faceless company who'd not failed before. It was easy to trust the teachers to make the right choices, because most people strived to do so. Trust was ingrained in Abigail, but when it came to trusting London, to trusting his actual intentions and desires, she'd fallen short. She erred on the side of protecting her emotions, and she'd obviously gotten it wrong. If she'd protected her actual self, then maybe she'd be in his arms now, folded up against him in his expansive bed, the feel of the luxurious sheets against her skin, the scent of him next to her. Skin on skin.

Abigail rested her head on her folded arms, against her knees.

"If I could only go home. If I could only go and stay alive. I'd put more trust where it was warranted, and less in where it was simply easy."

She thought she ought to pray, to think of her immortal soul. But even faced with her own mortality she was skeptical death was inevitable. To pray for heaven would be to admit escape was hopeless. And she still hoped. So she prayed for guidance. No bargaining; she honored God more than that and wasn't going to demean Him by acting as though anything she could give was worth His mercy.

Suddenly there was a scuffle in the room behind the thinnest wall, and a door on the other side opened and closed. She heard muttering but no conversation until the door opened and closed again.

In Japanese someone cried, "Get the safe!"

The response: "I am trying. It is heavy. Where should I bring it?"

"The car, the car! And then we must go. Now!"

"But they'll know we were here. There's too much left. Papers, plans for the schools in Korea, names, personal effects. The Nagoya girl is still here. Even if the documents were not found, the girl will tell them everything."

Silence, and Abigail leaned against the wall, pressing her ear to it. Translating was one thing, hearing it was another. They must have remembered her location and the possibility that she could understand the language.

"There is no time to discuss!"

"But if we leave everything, and leave *her*, we *will* be caught!"

There was a pregnant pause, full of decisions. Finally the response came, low and certain.

"Burn it all."

"What? We have no time. The police are coming up the road, the cameras saw the cars. Not just a car checking in. Lots of cars. They know. There's no time to pick and choose documents to fuel a bonfire!"

"Burn the whole house down."

"The . . . house?"

"It is wood, it will go quickly. Pour kerosene and burn it all. Do not question me. You do not have long, and we will need to leave."

The door shut and Abigail tripped backwards. The police were coming! They would find her! But the house . . .

Flames leapt in her imagination—this was surely not the end. This was surely not how she'd die.

She flung herself at the door, banging and shouting, then at the thin wall.

"Please let me out! Help! Help!"

Her energy was limitless now, fueled by adrenaline. The police were so close, the driveway was long, but it couldn't be more than a few minutes and they'd be pulling up. But a few minutes and the house would be on fire. They'd have to call the fire department, and who knew how long that would take?

She kicked, screamed, pounded with her fists. She tried each wall, even the thicker ones, in case someone might hear. Maybe Amy would be passing to meet them at the car and she'd hear. Maybe the police were already here.

Then there was a familiar scent, and an image of camping on the Colorado River as a child flashed into her mind. Gathering brush to start the fire, to pack the logs her parents had brought. The first smoke. The first flames.

The scent was far off, but grew thicker sooner than she'd expected. She kicked, shouted, and finally the room began to grow darker. The air grew smoky. Instructions from childhood flashed through her mind.

Feel the door with the back of your hand and if it's hot, don't open it. No, that was only if you *could* open the door.

If you're up high, drape a sheet or something from the window to alert rescuers. Of course, that was if you had a window and if your rescuers knew you were there. They had no idea she was in here, let alone where she was.

Stop, drop, and roll. No, that was if you were on fire.

Abigail choked back a sob. *Please not that.*

Stay close to the ground.

Abigail dropped down. Never had she been so glad to smell dirt. In comparison to the thickening smoke, the smell of dirt was more than welcome.

Heat rose around her, and she considered making another plea for help but to rise again into the smoke might mean when she came back down there would be no fresh air left.

It was going to happen anyway, running out of air. Abigail decided that instead of taking it laying down, literally, she'd fight as much as possible. She could only hope the fire trucks were there, or the police were in the house, or that someone would hear her.

Which wall? She could possibly only make it to one before the smoke filled her lungs. "The door," she breathed, cherishing the oxygen, knowing it wouldn't last. If someone was in any other room, against any other wall, they might hear her but not make it to the pantry in time to rescue her. She'd not have enough breath to shout directions anyway.

The smoke was filling the room quicker than she'd anticipated, and she crawled toward the door, her face close to the ground. Her nose and lips grazed the dirt, sucking in as much clean air as possible, until she reached the door.

Suddenly tears welled in Abigail's eyes. She had only minutes left, at best. Heat grew around her, and the line of light from the thin wall flickered; the room on the other side was on fire. This room would be next.

"London," she spoke to the floor. "I am so sorry . . ."

A newborn love that she'd paralyzed with her own pride and then analyzed to death. She'd give anything to see him again, to tell him she was sorry.

But she had nothing to give. Nothing except her last few breaths. She must act now.

Abigail choked back the tears, gathering all her courage to plunge up into the smoke and stand for the last time.

She sucked in as much air as she could, stood, and threw her weight into pounding on the door.

"HELP! HELP!"

No more "please." No sentences. Just a plea.

"HELP! HELP!"

And soon her lungs were empty. She pressed the last of the air out of them.

"HELP . . ."

Her body took over, and despite the smoke, she breathed in. Abigail choked, coughed, sputtered. She fell to the ground, trying to find a pocket of air where there was none. Against her will, her body breathed in again, drawing more thick smoke into her lungs.

Suddenly light filled the room, a bright, white light.

Abigail felt herself being lifted off the ground. She was moving, flying it felt, speeding past shapes and objects . . . and fire.

And then her ears filled with sounds sirens and shouts, her lungs with pure, clean air.

And, was she dreaming it? She rolled her head to the side and there was London, his face inches from hers, covered in ash and soot, a wet scarf tied around his nose and mouth.

She was lowered to the ground, yet London never stepped away, even as she was surrounded by paramedics.

"London," she whispered. It hurt to speak but it was exhilarating to draw clean air into her lungs.

"Shhh . . ."

People poked and prodded her, affixed an oxygen mask, asked her questions she couldn't hear. Her eyes were on London, and her heart was listening only for him.

⨏⨍

They had wanted her to stay in the hospital a little longer, but when London Crane insisted she be moved to The C Kauai where their team of private physicians would take care of her, the hospital staff did not argue. For one thing, this was London Crane, of all people. And for another, the staff on call for The C had better equipment and just as good training as those at the public hospital.

In London's suite at The C Kauai, Abigail settled back into the cool wine-colored bedding and allowed London to care for her. She'd answered questions for the police via notepad to rest her voice, and now, in his lush, mahogany room, she rested. It was a while before Abigail said anything other than his name; her throat was raw from the smoke.

Finally, as he was handing her a tray of soup and water—she could not get enough water—and a small glass of POG juice, she asked in a raspy voice, "Did they find them?"

London knew exactly what she meant. He pulled a chair up next to the bed.

"Shhhh. Please don't speak. Here, take a sip of water. Yes, they did. They caught them at a private airfield before the plane had even started its engines."

"All of them?" She took a sip of water.

"Inudori, Yamamoto, that woman Amy Hart, and one other man. The VP."

"Toru Ito," she coughed, and took another sip.

"Yes. All of them. Are you sure Amy didn't know they were planning on . . . well . . ."

"Murdering me?" Abigail shuddered. "No. She didn't. She knew about the school in South Korea. Not about the murders."

"Please, not so much."

London held a glass to her lips and she took one sip, then another.

"Abigail, I don't know how you had enough air to be shouting in that little room, but I'm so glad you did. I was running through the house—I knew you had to be there. I felt it. I would have had to leave soon—"

His voice caught with emotion. He swallowed the POG juice she offered him and continued.

"I was running out of air, too. I didn't know if I could will myself further, especially if you weren't there. It was my second biggest fear, that they'd taken you with them. My first was that you were there and that I wouldn't be able to find you."

"How did you know I hadn't joined them?"

"I saw your expression on the porch. You were shocked to see them, and I knew you wouldn't be happy about the situation, whatever it was. I saw your surprise. Yes, I followed you, but don't be mad—"

"I'm not."

"I went back to the police and told them who I'd seen at the plantation. They said they'd check it out. It wasn't a rush, though. It was economics—a Japanese school going under, and what business of theirs was it that some bigwigs were staying in town? Finally I told them I'd send my own security team down there, and they realized who I was, and sent people down. It was hours in the making, but finally they came down."

"You followed me?"

"You told me to let you make your own mistakes. I'd already reached my limit for rebuke. I didn't know the situation was dangerous. I just thought they were schmucks hiding out like that."

"The house—"

"Not burned down, but really gutted. That was no accident."

"No, they saw the police."

"On the road—I was in one of the cars—on the road we saw smoke far off. And when we got closer, flames. My stomach sank when I saw that house on fire. I just knew you were in there."

"Fire trucks—" Abigail started coughing, sipped some water, and coughed again.

"We called for them, but the station is far. I ran in, did a search of the rooms upstairs. But then the smoke was getting bad, and the flames started closing in. I went back outside for wet fabric to put around my mouth, and then I went back in. They were warning me not to. But I had to find you."

"A secret room . . ."

"Yes. I was looking behind every door. I even checked the pantry, but didn't find you. I was on my way out of the kitchen—it was getting too hot and I wanted to see if there was anywhere else I hadn't looked. I heard a shout. I heard you shout. A cry for help. With the smoke and flames, I couldn't tell where it was coming from. I went back into the pantry, just in case I missed something, and followed your cries for help to the back. The door was hidden really well. They'd even put a big bag of rice in front of it."

Rice? She hadn't been able to move a bag of rice? "Thought it was locked . . ."

"Oh, it was. But when I reached the door and heard your cries, well, heck, I guess it was adrenaline. I smashed it in."

"There you were on the ground. Hard to see you through all that smoke. I thought . . . But you'd just been shouting. I scooped you up and rushed out, not knowing if I were carrying you to safety or if you were already gone. But right when we stepped outside, you leaned into me, and I knew . . ."

His voice caught, and he touched her shoulder. Abigail threw her arms around his neck. She then pulled back the sheets and invited him in. She wanted to be as near him as possible.

To feel as alive as possible.

EPILOGUE

A warm, orange light flooded the low, wide window of the *tatami* room. Abigail yawned and rolled over, looking lazily out the window. The trees outside her window were every shade of green, red, brown and orange, contrasting with the clear blue of the autumn sky.

Her eyes scanned the expansive walls of the room; photo collages hung there of friends and family, and huge photo prints of Japan. As she dressed she examined the photos she passed by every day. The one over the dresser almost looked like an impressionist drawing of a tree from a distance, but as she got closer the details were revealed. She stood in jeans and a bright green t-shirt that read *Your World International School.* It had a smiling globe in the center. There was a group of elementary-school-aged children, also clad in bright green *Your World* t-shirts, surrounding her. Some made faces at the camera, others made a peace sign. One child sat on her shoulders and four more were hanging off her arms.

Near the door was one of her favorite photos. In the background of the photo stood the main temple room of Toganji—the temple she and London had temple-hopped to on one of their first outings several years back.

In the photo, London is wearing traditional Japanese clothing, with alternating black and grey stripes. Although he was trying to look serious, his aqua eyes were lit and his crooked smile was just beginning to form at the corners of his mouth.

Next to him stood Abigail, dressed in an ornate white kimono. Traditionally, Japanese women wear a white boxy hat with the kimono, but Abigail was anything but traditional. Instead, her black curls were left to their devices and she'd pinned fresh, white plum blossoms in her hair.

She laughed, remembering her wedding day. They had meant to take a traditional Japanese photo, with serious faces, but the excitement overtook them throughout the day and there was not one photo that was not teeming with energy and joy. The Japanese photographer had been apologetic for not capturing "an appropriate wedding photo," but Abigail and London had loved each and every photo.

Her phone summoned her from her memories. She checked the name and flipped it open.

"Hey, Saori."

"Hello, Abigail. I am sorry to call while you are still at home."

She glanced at the clock. There were still forty-five minutes until the morning kindergarten class started. "Is everything all right over there?"

The sound of children laughing and playing filled the other end of the line.

"Yes, everything at the school is well. I am calling to inform you that Cheryl's dentist appointment was cancelled today, so she is available to teach the morning class if you would like the morning off to have some fun!"

"Taking the morning off . . . well, that's tempting. But if she's teaching, is there anything you need from me?"

"Everything is set up fine, but to remind you, we will have the new student joining us today for the afternoon class and I cannot find the Your World tuition assistance forms. The family does not have the money for classes without the tuition assistance we offer."

"I have some copies of the forms here at home. You know, I'll just come in at the regular time and bring the forms. I could do some paperwork before the afternoon class. See you in twenty minutes."

Other than marrying the love of her life, opening Your World International was one of her greatest accomplishments. An English school for students who could not afford expensive *eikaiwas* like English World. Uncommon, but it worked.

When she'd returned to Japan with London five years ago, after the fire, he'd asked her what she planned to do next. She told him her dream for a school, and together they created a business plan. She'd hired on many of her previous teachers and, of course, Saori.

Together, they came up with a curriculum to teach English in a natural way to their students—the same way children acquire their first language. And while the original plan was to make it a charity-based school, it became so successful that they had students from all different income levels and were able to sustain themselves on income-based tuition alone.

She hurried down the mahogany stairs and into the office. She stopped in her tracks to see London's broad shoulders pulling off his bright green t-shirt, with waves of golden hair barely reaching the back of his neck. Even two years into their marriage, one look at him made her want to spend the entire day making love.

He swiveled around to face her, as though he were surprised to find her there. His aqua eyes followed the curves of her body and a crooked smile spread over his face. He'd heard her coming, and he was purposefully tempting her.

Abigail flipped open her phone. "Saori? Me again. I will be taking the morning off. I think I need to have a little fun."

ABOUT THE AUTHORS

Trisha Haddad is a San Diego writer whose passions include travel, reading, and spending time with her husband, Derek, and baby son. She is the author of *Best of Luck Elsewhere* (Genesis Press, 2009).

Monica Haddad is a 25-year-old writer living and working in Southern California. She earned her degree in Music Education, and spent the next two years teaching in Nagoya, Japan. She settled back into the States in 2009, where she spends her free time traveling, reading and enjoying the company of Eddie, her husband.

Trisha and Monica are not only sisters and friends, but have also been traveling companions in Asia, Europe, and the Mediterranean. Nihon Nights is their first collaborative fiction novel.

2011 Mass Market Titles

January

From This Moment
Sean Young
ISBN: 978-1-58571-383-7
$6.99

Nihon Nights
Trisha Haddad and Monica
  Haddad
ISBN: 978-1-58571-382-0
$6.99

February

The Davis Years
Nicole Green
ISBN: 978-1-58571-390-5
$6.99

Allegro
Patricia Knight
ISBN: 978-158571-391-2
$6.99

March

Lies in Disguise
Bernice Layton
ISBN: 978-1-58571-392-9
$6.99

Steady
Ruthie Robinson
ISBN: 978-1-58571-393-6
$6.99

April

The Right Maneuver
LaShell Stratton-Childers
ISBN: 978-1-58571-394-3
$6.99

Riding the Corporate Ladder
Keith Walker
ISBN: 978-1-58571-395-0
$6.99

May

Separate Dreams
Joan Early
ISBN: 978-1-58571-434-6
$6.99

I Take This Woman
Chamein Canton
ISBN: 978-1-58571-435-3
$6.99

June

Doesn't Really Matter
Keisha Mennefee
ISBN: 978-1-58571-434-0
$6.99

Inside Out
Grayson Cole
ISBN: 978-1-58571-437-7
$6.99

2011 Mass Market Titles (continued)
July

Rehoboth Road
Anita Ballard-Jones
ISBN: 978-1-58571-438-4
$6.99

Holding Her Breath
Nicole Green
ISBN: 978-1-58571-439-1
$6.99

August

The Sea of Aaron
Kymberly Hunt
ISBN: 978-1-58571-440-7
$6.99d

The Finley Sisters' Oath of
Romance
Keith Thomas Walker
ISBN: 978-1-58571-441-4
$6.99

September

October

November

December

Other Genesis Press, Inc. Titles

TRISHA HADDAD and MONICA HADDAD

Other Genesis Press, Inc. Titles (continued)

Blindsided	Tammy Williams	$6.99
Bliss, Inc.	Chamein Canton	$6.99
Blood Lust	J.M. Jeffries	$9.95
Blood Seduction	J.M. Jeffries	$9.95
Blue Interlude	Keisha Mennefee	$6.99
Bodyguard	Andrea Jackson	$9.95
Boss of Me	Diana Nyad	$8.95
Bound by Love	Beverly Clark	$8.95
Breeze	Robin Hampton Allen	$10.95
Broken	Dar Tomlinson	$24.95
Burn	Crystal Hubbard	$6.99
By Design	Barbara Keaton	$8.95
Cajun Heat	Charlene Berry	$8.95
Careless Whispers	Rochelle Alers	$8.95
Cats & Other Tales	Marilyn Wagner	$8.95
Caught in a Trap	Andre Michelle	$8.95
Caught Up in the Rapture	Lisa G. Riley	$9.95
Cautious Heart	Cheris F. Hodges	$8.95
Chances	Pamela Leigh Starr	$8.95
Checks and Balances	Elaine Sims	$6.99
Cherish the Flame	Beverly Clark	$8.95
Choices	Tammy Williams	$6.99
Class Reunion	Irma Jenkins/ John Brown	$12.95
Code Name: Diva	J.M. Jeffries	$9.95
Conquering Dr. Wexler's Heart	Kimberley White	$9.95
Corporate Seduction	A.C. Arthur	$9.95
Crossing Paths, Tempting Memories	Dorothy Elizabeth Love	$9.95
Crossing the Line	Bernice Layton	$6.99
Crush	Crystal Hubbard	$9.95
Cypress Whisperings	Phyllis Hamilton	$8.95
Dark Embrace	Crystal Wilson Harris	$8.95
Dark Storm Rising	Chinelu Moore	$10.95
Daughter of the Wind	Joan Xian	$8.95
Dawn's Harbor	Kymberly Hunt	$6.99
Deadly Sacrifice	Jack Kean	$22.95
Designer Passion	Dar Tomlinson Diana Richeaux	$8.95

Other Genesis Press, Inc. Titles (continued)

Do Over	Celya Bowers	$9.95
Dream Keeper	Gail McFarland	$6.99
Dream Runner	Gail McFarland	$6.99
Dreamtective	Liz Swados	$5.95
Ebony Angel	Deatri King-Bey	$9.95
Ebony Butterfly II	Delilah Dawson	$14.95
Echoes of Yesterday	Beverly Clark	$9.95
Eden's Garden	Elizabeth Rose	$8.95
Eve's Prescription	Edwina Martin Arnold	$8.95
Everlastin' Love	Gay G. Gunn	$8.95
Everlasting Moments	Dorothy Elizabeth Love	$8.95
Everything and More	Sinclair Lebeau	$8.95
Everything but Love	Natalie Dunbar	$8.95
Falling	Natalie Dunbar	$9.95
Fate	Pamela Leigh Starr	$8.95
Finding Isabella	A.J. Garrotto	$8.95
Fireflies	Joan Early	$6.99
Fixin' Tyrone	Keith Walker	$6.99
Forbidden Quest	Dar Tomlinson	$10.95
Forever Love	Wanda Y. Thomas	$8.95
Friends in Need	Joan Early	$6.99
From the Ashes	Kathleen Suzanne	$8.95
	Jeanne Sumerix	
Frost on My Window	Angela Weaver	$6.99
Gentle Yearning	Rochelle Alers	$10.95
Glory of Love	Sinclair LeBeau	$10.95
Go Gentle Into That Good Night	Malcom Boyd	$12.95
Goldengroove	Mary Beth Craft	$16.95
Groove, Bang, and Jive	Steve Cannon	$8.99
Hand in Glove	Andrea Jackson	$9.95
Hard to Love	Kimberley White	$9.95
Hart & Soul	Angie Daniels	$8.95
Heart of the Phoenix	A.C. Arthur	$9.95
Heartbeat	Stephanie Bedwell-Grime	$8.95
Hearts Remember	M. Loui Quezada	$8.95
Hidden Memories	Robin Allen	$10.95
Higher Ground	Leah Latimer	$19.95
Hitler, the War, and the Pope	Ronald Rychlak	$26.95
How to Kill Your Husband	Keith Walker	$6.99

Other Genesis Press, Inc. Titles (continued)

Other Genesis Press, Inc. Titles (continued)

Other Genesis Press, Inc. Titles (continued)

Path of Thorns	Annetta P. Lee	$9.95
Peace Be Still	Colette Haywood	$12.95
Picture Perfect	Reon Carter	$8.95
Playing for Keeps	Stephanie Salinas	$8.95
Pride & Joi	Gay G. Gunn	$8.95
Promises Made	Bernice Layton	$6.99
Promises of Forever	Celya Bowers	$6.99
Promises to Keep	Alicia Wiggins	$8.95
Quiet Storm	Donna Hill	$10.95
Reckless Surrender	Rochelle Alers	$6.95
Red Polka Dot in a World Full of Plaid	Varian Johnson	$12.95
Red Sky	Renee Alexis	$6.99
Reluctant Captive	Joyce Jackson	$8.95
Rendezvous With Fate	Jeanne Sumerix	$8.95
Revelations	Cheris F. Hodges	$8.95
Reye's Gold	Ruthie Robinson	$6.99
Rivers of the Soul	Leslie Esdaile	$8.95
Rocky Mountain Romance	Kathleen Suzanne	$8.95
Rooms of the Heart	Donna Hill	$8.95
Rough on Rats and Tough on Cats	Chris Parker	$12.95
Save Me	Africa Fine	$6.99
Secret Library Vol. 1	Nina Sheridan	$18.95
Secret Library Vol. 2	Cassandra Colt	$8.95
Secret Thunder	Annetta P. Lee	$9.95
Shades of Brown	Denise Becker	$8.95
Shades of Desire	Monica White	$8.95
Shadows in the Moonlight	Jeanne Sumerix	$8.95
Show Me the Sun	Miriam Shumba	$6.99
Sin	Crystal Rhodes	$8.95
Singing a Song…	Crystal Rhodes	$6.99
Six O'Clock	Katrina Spencer	$6.99
Small Sensations	Crystal V. Rhodes	$6.99
Small Whispers	Annetta P. Lee	$6.99
So Amazing	Sinclair LeBeau	$8.95
Somebody's Someone	Sinclair LeBeau	$8.95
Someone to Love	Alicia Wiggins	$8.95
Song in the Park	Martin Brant	$15.95
Soul Eyes	Wayne L. Wilson	$12.95

Other Genesis Press, Inc. Titles (continued)

Other Genesis Press, Inc. Titles (continued)

Order Form

Mail to: Genesis Press, Inc.
P.O. Box 101
Columbus, MS 39703

Name _____
Address _____
City/State _____ Zip _____
Telephone _____

Ship to (if different from above)
Name _____
Address _____
City/State _____ Zip _____
Telephone _____

Credit Card Information
Credit Card # _____ ☐ Visa   ☐ Mastercard
Expiration Date (mm/yy) _____ ☐ AmEx ☐ Discover

Qty.	Author	Title	Price	Total

Use this order	Total for books	_____
form, or call	**Shipping and handling:**	
	$5 first two books,	
	$1 each additional book	_____
1-888-INDIGO-1	Total S & H	_____
	Total amount enclosed	_____
	Mississippi residents add 7% sales tax